BEWARE!!
DO NOT READ THIS
BOOK FROM
BEGINNING TO END!

Enter the laboratories of the evil Dr. Eeek. These are labs with experiments so strange . . . so amazing . . . so *terrifying*! There are super-smart chimps and never-ending mazes. There are growling German shepherds and mind-boggling virtual reality. One visit with Dr. Eeek, and science class will seem like kindergarten!

The scary adventure is all about you. You decide what will happen. And you decide how terrifying the scares will be.

Start on page 1. Then follow the instructions at the bottom of each page. You make the choices.

If you make the right choices, you will escape from Dr. Eeek's deadly labs *alive*. If you make the wrong choice . . . BEWARE!

So take a long, deep breath, cross your fingers, and turn to page 1 to GIVE YOURSELF GOOSE-BUMPS!

READER BEWARE —
YOU CHOOSE THE SCARE!

Look for more
GIVE YOURSELF GOOSEBUMPS adventures
from R.L. STINE

R.L. STINE
GIVE YOURSELF

Goosebumps®

THE DEADLY EXPERIMENTS OF DR. EEEK

AN
APPLE
PAPERBACK

SCHOLASTIC INC.
New York Toronto London Auckland Sydney

A PARACHUTE PRESS BOOK

If you purchased this book without a cover, you should be aware that this book is stolen property. It was reported as "unsold and destroyed" to the publisher, and neither the author nor the publisher has received any payment for this "stripped book."

No part of this publication may be reproduced in whole or in part, or stored in a retrieval system, or transmitted in any form or by any means, electronic, mechanical, photocopying, recording, or otherwise, without written permission of the publisher. For information regarding permission, write to Scholastic Inc., 555 Broadway, New York, NY 10012.

ISBN 0-590-67318-1

Copyright © 1996 by Parachute Press, Inc. All rights reserved. Published by Scholastic Inc. APPLE PAPERBACKS and the APPLE PAPER-BACKS logo are registered trademarks of Scholastic Inc. GOOSEBUMPS is a registered trademark of Parachute Press, Inc.

12 11 10 9 8 7 6 5 4 3 2 1   6 7 8 9/9 0 1/0

Printed in the U.S.A.   40

First Scholastic Printing, February 1996

THE DEADLY EXPERIMENTS OF DR. EEEK

"How did you get in here?" a voice calls as you enter the waiting room at Eeek Laboratories. "That door is supposed to be locked at all times."

You and your friend Sam jump. You didn't think anyone was around.

Then you spot the receptionist sitting behind a tall desk. She's a short, frizzy-haired redhead wearing too much lipstick for her thin lips. She glares at you as if she expects you to turn around and leave — as soon as you figure out you're in the wrong place.

"I'm looking for my mom," you tell her.

"Who's your mom?" the receptionist asks. She starts to pack up her things to leave.

You glance at the clock. It's almost five-thirty — quitting time.

"She's the new lab technician," you explain. "She's working on some top secret experiments for Eeek."

"Really? For *Dr.* Eeek?" The receptionist gazes at you suspiciously.

"Yeah — I guess," you say.

But really, you're not sure. How come your mom never mentioned him before? Dr. Eeek? All she ever told you was that she had a new job in a *research* lab. You didn't know there was a *medical* doctor involved. Doctors give you the creeps.

Go on to PAGE 2.

"Are you *sure* your mom works for Dr. Eeek?" the receptionist grills you. She raises an eyebrow.

Her eyebrows give you the creeps.

In fact, this whole place gives you the creeps.

From the minute you stepped off the elevator on the nineteenth floor, there were no signs of life. No one in the echoing hall. Nothing but the creaking elevator door.

And then you spotted the door to Eeek Labs. Your mother never told you about that, either. The door looked like the door to a huge *vault*! It was heavy steel — and about six inches thick.

Your best friend Sam pulled a small handle near the edge of the door. To your surprise, the door swung open easily.

Okay, you told yourself. So the place has a weird door. That's no reason to freak out.

"Yeah, she works here," you tell the receptionist. "She does research."

"Well, take a seat," she replies. "I'm sure your mom will be right here." Then she packs up her oversized tote bag and walks out.

You search around for a chair. Then you see them. Across the room. The chairs are all orange plastic — and they're all chained together!

Sit down on PAGE 3.

You sit down in an orange plastic chair. But Sam doesn't. He starts roaming around the waiting room.

"So what movie is your mom going to take us to?" Sam asks.

You shrug. "Who knows? But remember, Sam — we promised my mom we wouldn't act *too* wild here," you warn with a grin.

"Yeah, yeah," he says. Like he really cares. He wanders over to the receptionist's desk. He picks up a glass of clear liquid that's sitting there.

It's probably just water, but . . .

"Hey!" you cry. "Don't drink that!"

But before you can stop him, he drinks it down. Sam drains the glass in one gulp.

Then he whirls around to face you.

"Sam! I mean it!" you moan. "We can't fool around. This is a *science* lab."

He starts to answer, but suddenly his face turns white. He clutches his throat and gasps. Then the veins on his neck start to pop out. A moment later, he makes a hideous face — as if he's turning into Dr. Jekyll and Mr. Hyde.

You freeze. Your heart pounds wildly.

"What did you drink?" you ask him.

Go on to PAGE 4.

You race over to the desk. You pick up the glass Sam was drinking from. And sniff to see if it has a smell. Nothing.

Sam bursts out laughing. He gives you a devilish grin.

"Water," Sam says, pointing at the glass. "It's just water!"

You can't help laughing, too. You like Sam. He's funny. But sometimes your best friend can go too far. He's always playing crazy jokes on you.

Sam gazes around. You're sure he's trying to find some other trouble to get into.

"Maybe we should look for my mom," you suggest.

Anything to keep Sam from getting into more trouble.

His eyes light up. "Great idea!" he cries. "Maybe we can do our own experiments!"

Uh . . . on second thought . . .

Maybe you should just sit tight and wait!

If you sit down and wait for your mom, turn to PAGE 11.

If you look for her, turn to PAGE 6.

"What am I doing?" Dr. Eeek repeats and then laughs. "You would never understand, my dear child."

Sam turns his head to stare at you. His eyes are filled with terror. "Get me out of here," he pleads.

"There is no way for your friend to save you," Dr. Eeek tells Sam. Then he walks over to the scary machine and starts turning dials. Something buzzes. Something else hums.

"Help me," Sam cries. "Please. Help!"

A moment later, the jar of pickles starts to glow.

"Stop!" you scream. You lunge at Dr. Eeek.

But Dr. Eeek thrusts out a hand to stop you. He's strong — even if he is an old guy.

"Give up," Dr. Eeek commands.

But you don't give up. You run over to the table and rip the wires off Sam's feet. Then you grab his arm.

"Let's run!" you say to your friend. Dr. Eeek throws back his head and laughs.

"Ha! You'll *never* get out of here. Never!" he bellows. "All the exits are locked. Unless . . ."

Unless what? Find out on PAGE 76.

"Let's go look for my mom," you tell Sam. "But remember — no goofing around. This is a science lab."

"Right," Sam agrees. He zooms through the waiting room door into a long hallway. You quickly follow.

Hmmm. The hallway is pretty boring. Just a lot of closed doors on both white walls. And there's no way to know what's behind most of them.

You open the first one and peek in.

Bummer. It's just the lounge. At least that's what it looks like. There are two beat-up brown couches, a table, some chairs, and a bunch of vending machines.

"Got any change?" Sam asks. "I'm starving."

You pull out coins from your pocket. You've got enough for only one snack selection. You drop the coins into the slot in the machine. You start to punch the number of your favorite candy bar.

But before you can hit the buttons, a hand suddenly clamps down on your shoulder!

Turn around slowly on PAGE 14.

You stare at the thing under the covers. Your heart beats triple time.

What is it? A boy? A dog?

Or a little bit of each?

"Help me," he says again. "Please. My name is Joseph. Dr. Eeek tried to turn me into a German shepherd, but it didn't work. So now he's trying to turn me back into a kid."

You don't know what to say. This is so creepy — so sick! How could your mother work in a place like this?

"I'm strapped down," the boy explains. He gestures toward his hairy, doggy arms. "Loosen the straps so I can get free."

"Okay," you say. Your stomach lurches at the sight of bristly dog hair all over this kid's body.

You start to undo the straps. But before you can finish, you hear footsteps approaching.

Quick! You'd better find a place to hide!

If you hide in Dr. Eeek's office on the other side of the room, turn to PAGE 129.

If you hide under the operating table, turn to PAGE 74.

"We're stuck — in Dr. Eeek's lab," you agree. "Unless you can reprogram Dr. Eeek's computer."

"No problem," Sam says. "I learned how to do that at summer camp. We've just got to find the computer room!"

Hey — you *knew* there was a reason you liked Sam so much!

You and Sam slap each other high fives. Then you race back to the lab. Dr. Eeek is still out cold on the floor.

Sam sits down at the computer console and starts typing.

This is weird! you think. In reality, you and Sam are *still* sitting in the black leather chairs. Strapped in. Watching this virtual reality game.

But in the game, you're reprogramming Dr. Eeek's computer — so you can get out of here!

Sam changes the program in minutes. Now the game has everything — the eighteenth floor, your mom, and even the police department. It's located right across the street from Eeek Labs.

Once again, you and Sam race down the hall. Punch the elevator buttons. Zip down to the eighteenth floor. Find your mom. And call the police.

Then the picture in your headset goes totally blank!

Turn to PAGE 51.

"Okay, okay!" you scream. "I'll do it! Just get this stuff off me!"

Then you shut your lips tight. The goo has crept up your throat and over your chin. It's almost into your mouth.

You can't tell whether it's the goo making your throat feel tight — or the fear.

All you know is that you can't breathe.

Sam claws at the goo, trying to pull it off his neck. He accidentally hits his nose, and the goo goes in it.

"Hurry!" you scream through your clenched teeth and tight lips.

Then you squeeze your eyes shut. If the goo is going to choke you, you don't want to see it coming.

Hurry to PAGE 24.

As soon as the door is locked, the chimps stop playing games and reading books. The fun and games are over. Several of them run to the windows and pull down the shades.

Then Oscar takes a lab coat from a hook on the wall — and slips it on!

He pulls something from the pocket and puts it in his palm. Then he walks over to Professor Yzark and holds out his hand.

Resting there is a small chocolate treat.

Professor Yzark snatches it and stuffs it in his mouth — as if it's a reward! Oscar pats him on the head. Then Oscar points to a far corner of the room.

Hey — you didn't see that before!

The whole wall is lined with large cages!

"Eeek! Eeek!" Oscar cries, making that same sound again.

Professor Yzark obediently hurries over to one of the cages. He crawls inside, lies down, and curls up to take a nap.

"Uh-oh . . ." Sam croaks, clutching your arm. "Look!"

Turn to PAGE 45!

"Let's not mess around," you say to Sam. "We should wait for my mom."

You take a seat in one of the orange plastic chairs in the waiting room. Sam plops down in another one.

"Bummer," he says. "I thought your mom was going to take us to the movies."

"She is," you assure him. "As soon as she gets off work."

But you look at your watch and think, Uh-oh. She's late again. This has happened a lot lately. You hardly ever see your mom since she started working at Eeek Labs. She spends more and more time at the lab. When you complained about it this morning, she apologized and gave you a big hug. She offered to take you to dinner and the movies that night. "And bring Sam, if you want," she said.

You check your watch again. It's almost six o'clock. Where is she?

Suddenly the door opens. A short woman in a white lab coat steps into the waiting room. She stares at you and Sam. Then she motions for you to come with her.

"Sorry. We've been running late," the woman says. "I'm Vanessa. Follow me."

Turn to PAGE 12.

"You're here for the Raster experiment, aren't you?" Vanessa asks. "The pay is fifty dollars *cash*. You get it at the end of the experiment. And it takes only about twenty minutes. Let's go."

You look at Sam. Fifty dollars?

But what kind of experiment is it?

If you go along with Vanessa, turn to PAGE 20.

If you don't want to take a chance on the Raster experiment, turn to PAGE 63.

You want to scream, but nothing comes out.

The chimp moves closer. Closer to your throat.

But he doesn't grab you. Or even touch you. Instead, he reaches past you — to the buttons on the candy machine. He points directly at A-6.

"Hey!" cries Sam. "He wants you to get a different candy bar!"

"Cool," you say, smiling at this amazing monkey. "But is it okay to give candy to a chimp?"

Before you can decide, Sam pushes the buttons for A-6. A chocolatey-peanuty thing drops into the slot. Sam quickly unwraps the candy bar and hands it to the chimpanzee.

His monstrous teeth chomp down — *hard* — on the candy. He finishes it in two bites — and then pats you on the head.

A moment later, he motions for you to follow him.

"Come on! Let's see what he wants!" Sam cries.

"I don't know," you reply. "I thought we were looking for my mom. Maybe we should go back to the waiting room."

Sam rolls his eyes. "Where's your sense of adventure?"

Well? Where *is* your sense of adventure?

If you follow the chimp, turn to PAGE 101.

If you go back to the waiting room, turn to PAGE 42.

"Wow!" you gasp, as you turn around.

It's a big hairy chimpanzee!

You and Sam freeze. This chimp has you cornered in the lounge. Where did he come from? Is he friendly? Or dangerous? You have no idea what he'll do.

And he's bigger than any chimp you've ever seen.

In fact, he's at least as tall as you are. More like a gorilla, you think. You swallow hard.

"I've never seen a chimp up close like this before," Sam whispers.

"Me, neither," you whisper back.

The chimp tilts his head, staring at you. He never seems to blink.

Then slowly he reaches his other big hairy hand — toward your throat!

Turn back to PAGE 13.

"Uh — can I help you?" you ask the teenager, as you open the front door.

"Chimp," he grunts in a deep voice. "Got him?"

Before you can say anything, Oscar rushes right past you. He flings himself into the guy's arms. He strokes the guy's long hair and playfully pats him on the face. Then the two of them start making chimp sounds — as if they know each other!

"Thanks," the guy says, flashing you a smile. All at once he vaults over your porch railing with Oscar in his arms. He leaps into his waiting Jeep and drives off.

"Wait!" you scream, running after them.

This can't be the guy the professor sent — can it?

Then you see the guy's license plate. It's one of those vanity plates — the kind that spells out a sentence or word.

You stare, mouth hanging open, at the simple black letters.

No one is going to believe this, you realize. Not when you tell them the chimp was picked up by a tanned, half-naked guy who grunted and drove a car with a license plate that read:

T A R Z A N

Nah. Don't even think it.

No way. Couldn't be.

Could it?

THE END

Dr. Eeek is holding you tight by your right wrist. So you take a swing with your left and try to smack him. You miss.

You kick at him and start yelling. "Sam! Sam!" you shout.

Dr. Eeek shoves you out into the hall before Sam can reach you. Down the corridor. Into yet another lab room.

How many rooms does this place have, anyway? Plenty!

This one is filled with mirrors — on the walls, the floor, and the ceiling. There's a big red switch on the inside of the door.

Still holding your wrist, Dr. Eeek pulls the switch.

You hear a buzzing sound. Then a crackle. Then a flash of light so bright, so intense, you think you're going to be blinded forever. It's like the glare from a super-huge flashbulb on the world's biggest camera.

The light shuts off. But you still can't see for several minutes. Finally your eyes return to normal. You look in the mirror.

Hey — where are you? All you can see is a hundred reflections of Dr. Eeek. Dr. Eeek . . . holding on to Dr. Eeek's wrist!

Wait a minute. Wasn't he holding onto *your* wrist?

Figure this out on PAGE 50.

You clear your throat.

"Uh, actually, I've got to go," you say to Dr. Eeek. "I've got to meet my mom."

"I'm staying," Sam announces.

Dr. Eeek shrugs. "As you wish," he says to you. "Good-bye. Pleasant meeting you."

You glare at Sam and motion toward the door. But he won't follow you.

You step out into the hallway alone.

You start toward the reception area. But then you hear a voice cry out.

"Help! Someone help me!"

You freeze. Was that Sam? Did the sound come from behind you? Or was it in front of you? You can't be sure.

An instant later, you hear the cry again.

If you go back and check on Sam, run to PAGE 81.

If you think someone else might be in trouble, hurry to PAGE 99.

You quickly turn left. And stare at six German shepherds racing toward you in the Canine Maze. Three come at you from one side. Three from the other. You're trapped!

Their needle-sharp teeth drip with saliva. Two of them froth at the mouth. One of them has caked, dried blood all over its face.

As if it had eaten raw meat — or *something* — earlier today.

Don't scream, you tell yourself. Don't show fear. And don't run.

But what can you do?

There's only one way to call off the dogs — with a silver whistle.

But do you have one?

If you met the half-boy, half-dog and got a silver whistle from him, turn to PAGE 127.

If not, turn to PAGE 110.

All of a sudden, the sprinklers turn on. Hard.
VERY hard.

In fact, the water gushes out so fast, it almost
knocks you down. You stumble. Your foot slips
off the chair.

GLUG. Water fills your mouth. Instantly,
you're not only soaking wet — you're almost
drowning!

What's happening? you ask yourself as you spit
water. You stand up and gaze around the reception area.

Oh, no! you realize. Water is gushing out of the
sprinkler so fast, the room is filling up!

Within minutes, you're ankle-deep in water —
and it's quickly rising.

You can't *believe* how fast the water pours out.
It's more like Niagara Falls than like a sprinkler!

You gulp — and then suddenly you know the
truth. This is another one of Dr. Eeek's traps!

The room seems to be watertight. And the
water is rising.

Rising.

It's up to your knees. . . .

---

*Close your mouth and hold your nose until you
get to PAGE 79.*

"Fifty bucks?" Sam exclaims. His eyes light up.

"Great," you say, grinning. "What do we have to do?"

"Dr. Eeek will explain it to you," Vanessa replies mysteriously. "Follow me."

You follow Vanessa into a long hallway. The place is empty — eerily empty. Closed doors line both sides of the hall. Vanessa's high heels click on the tile floor as she leads the way.

Where is she taking you?

Finally she stops in front of a door with triple locks. There's an intercom box on the wall beside the door. She pushes the button.

"Yes?" a man's voice crackles.

"They're here," Vanessa announces.

Why is she acting as if they were expecting you?

Click. You hear an electronic lock unlocking. Then another. And another. The door swings open. You peer into the room. It's pitch-black.

"Come in," a voice says from the darkness.

Find out what's waiting for you on PAGE 32.

You get a sinking feeling in your gut, as the message sinks in.

You're on the wrong floor. Your mom's lab is downstairs!

"I'll give you one chance," Dr. Eeek says as the goo starts creeping back up your face. "One chance to either escape — or find the antidote."

The antidote? You mean there's something that will reverse the effects of the goo? A way to make this stuff stop growing all over you?

"Twenty seconds left," Dr. Eeek warns. Then he closes his eyes and starts to count.

"One, two, three . . ."

He's counting pretty fast.

If you search the lab for an antidote, hurry to PAGE 128.

If you buy more time by smearing goo all over Dr. Eeek's real face, turn to PAGE 73.

You decide to look under the sheet. Why not? It can't be that bad. Can it?

Trembling, you walk over to the operating table. Sweat beads on your forehead.

But you've got to do it. You've got to pull back that sheet.

Slowly, you lift just a corner of the sheet. You peek underneath. Near the head. Or at least you hope it's the head. It's the opposite side from the sneaker, anyway.

Then you lift the sheet just a little more.

Then more.

"No!" you scream when you spot what's underneath the stained cover.

"Help me!" cries a boy about your age.

Or at least you *think* it's a boy.

You can't really tell — because half of his body is covered in fur!

Turn to PAGE 7.

"Dogs?" you say. "But I thought . . ."

"What did you think?" Dr. Eeek asks coldly.

"I, uh . . . well, I thought this was a maze that you usually used for dogs," you say. "To train them, or something. I thought we had to find our way out. But I didn't think the dogs would be in there with us at the same time!"

"You just didn't *think*," Dr. Eeek says briskly. "Ah, well. Too bad."

He crosses his arms over his chest and stares at you.

This conversation is over.

"Oh, well," Sam groans. "Come on. What are we waiting for? The sooner we go, the sooner we'll get out of here."

Sam's right, you decide. Except that you keep remembering what Dr. Eeek said.

Beware of the dogs. Beware of the dogs. Beware of the dogs.

You step into the maze corridor. There's a strange smell in the air. Like a dog smell. It makes the hair on the back of your neck stand up.

Creep down the hall on PAGE 31.

All at once, you hear a buzzing sound.

You open your eyes. Dr. Eeek is holding some kind of electronic wand device in his hands. The device is about eight inches long and two inches thick — about the size of a battery-powered screwdriver.

He passes the wand in the air over the goo, without touching it. Immediately the goo begins to fall away from your arms, your hands, your face.

Whew! Close one, you think.

You'd like to yank open the door and run like crazy. But you've still got to wait for Sam.

Dr. Eeek passes the buzzing wand over Sam. Within seconds, the goo is gone for good.

Or rather, it's lying in a puddle on the lab floor.

Dr. Eeek gathers it up in his hands. He molds the goo into a giant sticky wad the size of a basketball.

"How did you do that?" Sam asks. The goo didn't stick to Dr. Eeek's hands!

"Never mind," Dr. Eeek says. "Follow me."

Follow him to PAGE 28.

"Okay," you give in. "We'll do it. What do we have to do?"

Dr. Eeek just smiles slightly. Then he motions for you to follow him.

"This way," he orders.

He leads you down a long hall, with doors on both sides. He stops short at a door painted green.

"What's in there?" you whisper to Sam.

"I don't know," Sam says. "Some kind of experiment, probably."

Yeah. Probably, you think.

Until Dr. Eeek pulls open the door.

Go to PAGE 56.

Okay.

Let's be clear. You want to worm your way out of this mess. Which means you want another chance to face the evil-minded, twisty-faced Dr. Eeek.

Right?

Right.

Sounds reasonable.

So all you have to do is prove one of the following:

A) You'll break out in hives if you read the words **THE END** one more time in the next five minutes.

B) You know the difference between creepy, spooky, and scary — and you can spell all three correctly.

C) Between you and your best friend, you've read every single GOOSEBUMPS book in existence — and you haven't had nightmares once.

If you can honestly claim A, B, or C — congratulations! You get to start again — and make a better choice — on PAGE 17. (Hint: Help Sam this time.)

If not, turn to PAGE 104.

"Let go!" you shout at the octopus. You grab at a spear that's hanging near the edge of the oversized tank. You jab the octopus with the spear. The huge, gray-black tentacle jerks back. Then you reach in the tank and jab the tentacle around Sam's neck.

Inky black liquid squirts out into the water. For a moment, you can't see a thing.

Then all at once, Sam bobs to the surface.

"Thanks!" he shouts. You give him a hand out of the tank.

The two of you dry off, using towels that seem to be waiting for you. Then Sam ducks into a locker room to find a change of clothes. While he's gone, Dr. Eeek walks into the room.

Hey — isn't this still virtual reality? What's *he* doing here?

"Well, well, well," Dr. Eeek says. "How are we doing, people? Having a nice swim?"

Oh, no! You suddenly get it. You've got to defeat Dr. Eeek *here* — in the virtual reality game! On his own turf!

You try to dodge and run around him. But he grabs you on the wrist. Your *right* wrist. You were planning to slug him.

Now what are you going to do?

If you are right-handed, turn to PAGE 16.
If you are left-handed, turn to PAGE 88.

Dr. Eeek leads you into an adjoining room. Two big black leather chairs with padded headrests stand side by side. The chairs look like airplane cockpit console seats. They sit all alone in the middle of the empty, darkened room, facing a two-way mirror.

Then you notice something. Each chair has a headset on the seat. Like the headgear Sam has with his virtual reality game.

"Have a seat," Dr. Eeek instructs, pointing. He clearly wants you to take the seat on the right. He points Sam to the chair on the left. "And put on the headsets."

You're about to sit down when you notice something else.

Straps. On the arms of the chairs.

It looks as if he's planning to strap you in!

If you sit down and put on the headset, turn to PAGE 35.

If you'd rather get out of there — FAST! — run to PAGE 113.

You and Sam run down the hall to the canine lab.

Luckily, Dr. Eeek is nowhere to be seen.

Then you spot something that makes your heart leap into your throat. Your mom's *other* shoe! It's lying on the floor, wedged in the opening of another door. Across from the operating room.

In small black letters, a sign on the door reads: CANINE MAZE. You pick up the shoe and push the door open.

Instantly, the sound of snarling, growling, barking dogs fills your ears.

"Weird!" Sam says, staring into the Canine Maze hallway.

Straight ahead, you see a twisting, turning corridor. Much narrower than a regular hall.

And then you see her. Your mom!

She's trapped at the end of that narrow hall — surrounded by five angry German shepherds!

They've got her pinned against the wall.

And they're moving in for the kill!

Quick! Do something before they turn her into *chomped* meat!

Sprint to PAGE 59.

"There's got to be a way out — doesn't there?" Sam cries.

"I don't know. I can't remember what Dr. Eeek said. Maybe the maze just goes around and around in circles — forever!" you shriek. "Maybe we'll die of starvation. Or run out of air. Maybe the only way out is that door back there — the one he just locked."

You and Sam don't say anything for the next few minutes. But you're both beginning to sweat. The worst part is the silence in the maze. The dead silence. It doesn't even echo a little. The only sound is the sound of your sneakers — and Sam's thick hiking boots — on the tile floor.

And the smell. That doggy smell. It's getting stronger.

And stronger.

Then all at once you come to a fork. A choice. The maze corridor goes either left or straight ahead.

You look left. You see only a short piece of hallway and then another turn.

Straight ahead, the hallway seems to stretch on for a long, long time without turning.

Which way?

To go left, turn to PAGE 18.
To go straight, turn to PAGE 130.

You take a few more steps forward — farther into the maze.

BLAM!

The door slams shut behind you with a clang.

Now you really *are* trapped.

"Which way?" Sam asks.

"Don't be dumb," you snap. "We haven't come to a choice yet. Just keep going straight."

You continue walking. The hallway twists and turns five times. Left. Right. Right. Left. Left again, but at an angle. Still, you aren't exactly lost. You could easily turn around and go back the way you came.

But your heart pounds wildly. You feel like an animal caught in a trap. Just knowing that it's a maze — that there's only one way out. . . .

Then it hits you. "Hey," you call to Sam, swallowing hard. Your voice sounds high. You hope Sam doesn't notice how freaked out you are. "Did Dr. Eeek actually say there was a way *out* of here?"

Go on to PAGE 30.

You step into the dark room. A light flashes on.

"Well, well, well. What have we here?" says an older man in a white lab coat. He has gray hair and a soft, pudgy face.

"Our next two appointments," Vanessa explains. She tucks a strand of her long brown hair behind her ear. "They're here for the Raster experiment."

"Really?" the man says. He pushes his wrinkled face right up to within an inch of your nose. He stares you in the eye.

You try to gaze away. There's something odd about him. About one of *his* eyes. It looks as if his right cheek has been pulled up to meet the eye — and been stapled there. It gives him a weird squint.

Then you notice something else. His lab coat is on backward.

"I'm Dr. Eeek. Are you sure you're here for the Raster experiment?" the man asks.

"Yeah — definitely," Sam insists. "What do we have to do?"

"That all depends," Dr. Eeek says with an evil-sounding laugh. "What are you *willing* to do?"

Decide on PAGE 64.

You stare at your image in the chrome panel.

The goo has grown up over your nose, eyes, hair — and all the way down the back of your head. In fact, it covers every inch of the top half of your body.

From the waist up, you're green and sticky-gooey. You look like a creature from a cheap sci-fi film. From the waist down, you look like a regular kid.

Luckily, the goo doesn't choke you. You can breathe through it — and you can see. It just makes everything look green.

When the elevator reaches the next floor, the doors open. And your *mom* gets on!

"Mom! Hi!" you try to say. Only the sound doesn't come out.

"Aahhhhh!" she screams, spotting you and Sam. "Aliens from outer space!"

And she calls herself a scientist?

Well, bad news. If your own mother thinks you're an alien, what do you think the United States military is going to do when they get a look at you?

That's right. It's time to learn how to say, "Wrxt Rinp" — which is Martian for . . .

THE END

You decide to hide in Dr. Eeek's office. You run in, shut the door, and lock it.

You duck down, so you can't be seen through the office window. The feeling of being hunted is terrifying. Your heart races a mile a minute.

CLOMP. CLOMP.

Someone's coming. You can hear his footsteps getting closer. Closer.

He is in the operating room now. You hear him bump into the metal table that the half-dog, half-boy is lying on.

CRASH! Metal instruments clatter and clang to the floor.

"Clumsy me," Dr. Eeek says. "Excuse me, Joseph. I hope I didn't hurt your hand . . . er . . . paw . . . just then."

Your heart pounds even harder. What if Dr. Eeek comes into his office?

Turn to PAGE 57.

You and Sam sit in the black leather chairs. Dr. Eeek places the headsets on you and straps you both in. The visor-goggles on the headset cover your eyes. Everything is dark.

Then you hear Dr. Eeek's footsteps. He's walking over to a console. He punches keys on a keyboard. All at once, your headset pops to life.

"Amazing!" you cry, staring at the graphics in your visor.

In the headset, you see a virtual reality scene that is so lifelike — it's even *better* than reality! Even though you are strapped in a chair, it feels as if you are really there.

Where?

Hawaii — or some kind of tropical South Seas island. You see yourself walking along a rocky cliff near a lagoon. Palm trees sway all around. Tropical birds are everywhere. The air is soft and warm. The water is turquoise blue. You wonder what it would be like to jump into that beautiful water — seventy feet below.

Uh-oh. Watch out — your thoughts are controlling this game! In the next instant, you start to fall . . . fall . . .

"Aaaaaahhhhhh!" you scream at the top of your lungs.

You are about to smack your head on the rocks below!

Go to PAGE 43.

"I haven't done a thing to your mother," Dr. Eeek says. "But you see, you've made a terrible mistake. Your mother doesn't work here at Eeek Labs. She works at EIK Labs — elsewhere in this building. So if you ever want to see her again, you'll have to get out of my laboratory." He gives you a slow, wicked smile. "And I'm afraid that just isn't likely to happen. Unless . . ."

Unless what? Find out on PAGE 76.

Help Dr. Eeek with the Raster experiment?

"No way, you creep!" you shout at Dr. Eeek. "You're not going to experiment on us!"

Then you lunge at him with your gooey hands. You try to smear some of the goo on him.

It sticks to his hands — but it doesn't seem to bother him.

"Ha, ha, ha!" Dr. Eeek shouts, tossing his head back and roaring with laughter.

What's so funny, you wonder.

You're not laughing. The green goo is creeping into your nose now. You glance over at Sam. He seems to be in a trance. The goo is covering his mouth.

Neither of you can breathe!

Find out what's so funny on PAGE 44.

Right away, you know you're in an operating room.

Tiled walls, metal cabinets, steel sink. Heart monitors. Cabinets full of rubber gloves. Surgical lights above a stainless steel operating table. Lumpy objects under a stained hospital sheet.

Wait a minute.

Lumpy objects under a stained hospital sheet?

Hurry to PAGE 47.

Stay cool, you try to tell yourself. But you can't. Your blood is pumping through your veins at one hundred miles an hour.

All you can think is: The phone went dead! Dr. Eeek must have cut the lines! Now you'll never get out of here — unless you come up with another plan. QUICK!

And then you remember Sam. Strapped in that black leather chair. Trapped in some horrible version of virtual reality. Clutching his throat.

And screaming for his life!

Suddenly you glance up at the ceiling and notice the emergency sprinkler system. The ones that turn on by themselves during a fire. Hey — maybe there's a way to trigger those sprinklers — and bring the fire department to the lab!

On the other hand, that could take a long time. And time is something you don't have.

Maybe you should run back to the lab where Sam is trapped. And try to save him yourself. In the virtual reality game,

What do you think?

If you set off the sprinklers, turn to PAGE 114.
If you run back to the room with the black leather chairs, have a seat on PAGE 105.

Maybe you'd better lie down, you decide.

Your knees feel so weak, you can hardly stand. You glance around for someplace to sit. But there isn't anything.

"Oh, well," you say, as you stretch out right there on Dr. Eeek's operating room floor!

Within seconds, you feel your eyes closing. Suddenly you're so tired. You've just got to get some sleep. And maybe then . . .

ZZZZZZZZZZ. You're out like a light.

Snoring away.

A few hours later, you open your eyes again.

"Mom!" you cry, sitting straight up in bed. In bed?

No. It can't be true. But you gaze around — and it *is* true! You're home in your own bed.

You blink once. Twice. How'd you get here?

"Wow, you must have been having a terrible dream," your mom says. "You were talking and moaning all night in your sleep."

You mean this was *all* just a dream? It never happened?

"Anyway, why don't you visit my new lab today," your mom goes on. "Come right after school. I'll show you around. Then we'll go to dinner and a movie. And bring Sam."

Uh-oh. Here you go again!

THE END

Dr. Eeek leads you down a long white hallway. Doors line both walls. All the doors are closed, which gives you the creeps. What's going on behind them?

Finally Dr. Eeek opens a door on the right. G-LAB is printed on the door.

"Is this your mom's lab?" Sam whispers.

"Who knows?" you whisper back.

"Right this way," Dr. Eeek instructs. He stands aside so that you and Sam can enter first. Inside, the room is crowded with all the standard lab equipment. Tables, sinks, beakers, Bunsen burners. Jars of strange-looking things.

But your mom is nowhere in sight.

Then you notice a blob of thick, oozy green stuff sitting on one of the black lab counters. It looks like a cross between minty toothpaste gel and Silly Putty. It's the size of a Jell-O softball.

And it's glowing softly.

"What's that?" Sam asks, pointing at the green goo.

"This?" Dr. Eeek says. He picks up the blob. "Here — catch!"

He tosses the blob of goo right at you!

Catch it on PAGE 96.

"We'd better not mess around," you tell Sam as you back away from the chimp. "Let's go back to the waiting room. I mean it — now!"

Reluctantly, Sam follows you. The two of you watch the chimp the whole time you back out of the room.

When you reach the door, the chimp tilts his head to one side and waves good-bye. He looks really sad to see you leave!

Then you hurry back down the hall to the waiting room. It's still empty. But a moment later, the main door — the one that looks like a vault door — swings all the way open. And your mom sweeps in.

"*There* you are!" she exclaims. "I was afraid this would happen. You're in the wrong waiting room! Come on."

She nods her head toward the elevators in the hall.

"What movie are we going to see?" you ask.

"We're too late for the movies now," she says. "I think we'll just go home and go to bed."

BORING!

See what happens when you have no sense of adventure?

THE END

With all your might, you try to throw your body away from the rocks.

It works — but just barely. You almost graze the rocks as you drop directly into the lagoon. You sink for a minute. Then you give a kick and shoot back to the top.

Good thing you can swim!

You climb out of the water and sit on the rocks to dry off. The sun warms you. Pretty soon your clothes are nearly dry.

This is freaky! you think to yourself. If it's just a virtual reality game, why do you actually *feel* so damp?

Then you hear a rustling sound in the bushes. Before you can jump up, a ten-foot-long Komodo dragon darts out at you!

You scream. You've read enough about Komodo dragons to know how dangerous they are. They're the world's largest living lizards! And they're fast, too. This guy could jump at you, chomp down on your stomach with his jagged teeth, and kill you in a flash.

You can't decide whether to freeze or run.

But you'd better decide something — and fast!

Freeze on PAGE 75.
Or run like crazy to PAGE 86.

Slowly, Dr. Eeek takes his right hand and begins to pick at a spot on his left wrist — just above the gob of goo you smeared on him.

You gasp. He's pulling off his skin!

No, you realize. He's pulling off a thin, lifelike rubber flesh-colored glove — a glove that looks exactly like his real hand.

So that's why the goo didn't hurt him!

A moment later, he reaches up and pulls off a skintight, lifelike mask that's covering his face.

"No!" you shout when you see his real face. It's not the same face as the mask. Instead, he has the pasty, pudgy face of a man your mom once showed you in a picture. A man who was fired from her lab — for being totally crazy!

"You're Herbert Wimplemeyer, the crazed scientist!" you try to shout.

But the green goo is creeping into your mouth. His name comes out sounding like "Werbert Dumplemurr."

"I *hate* it when people can't pronounce my name!" Dr. Eeek growls.

Turn to PAGE 119.

As you stare at the cages, you get a horrible sinking feeling. You see that several of the cages are occupied. But not by chimps.

By *people*! They're all adults. Most of them are wearing lab coats. And all of them are asleep.

Sam jabs you in the ribs and points. That woman curled up in the cage in the corner — it's the thin-lipped receptionist!

No wonder the halls of Eeek Laboratories were so empty!

"Hey, what's going on here?" Sam shouts.

Oscar smiles at you. A chimp smile. Then he lets out a series of *eeks*.

You can't understand chimpanzee. But if you could, you'd hear Oscar saying: "We're studying human brains. Humans are very smart. And physically they're a lot like chimpanzees. There is much we can learn from them." Then he pats you on the head. "We're especially delighted that we now have two human children to study," he goes on. "It should be very interesting!"

You and Sam back away. You don't understand what he just said. But as you stumble into the locked door, you're pretty sure you understand one very important scientific fact. This is definitely . . .

THE END

It works!

The German shepherds stop charging at you!

You're doing it! You're making them back down! One by one, the German shepherds turn around and run the other way.

"Let's follow them. Maybe they know a way out!" you want to say to Sam. But you can't talk. You're still a human being inside. But you've got the body of a dog!

And then you think: Wait a minute. Why follow them? They're just dogs.

You and Sam have got to find a way to turn yourselves back into kids again!

You watch the dogs for a minute. They really seem to know their way around this maze.

Well, which is it?

Do you want to follow the dogs?

Or wander the maze by yourselves?

If you follow the dogs, turn to PAGE 123.

If you wander the maze by yourselves, turn to PAGE 52.

You're afraid to look under the sheet — and afraid not to. What is that lumpy object? Is *that* what was crying out for help?

You peer closer — and notice a kid's sneaker poking out from under the sheet!

You feel so light-headed. You think you'd better lie down.

But where?

No way are you going to lie down in the operating room!

"Help," a weak voice says. "Please — help me."

You swallow hard. Your heart pounds. The room begins to spin.

Do you dare look under that sheet?

If you look under the sheet, turn to PAGE 22.
If you think you'd better lie down first, turn to PAGE 40.

48

You break out in hives.

Little bumps pop out all over your body. On your face. Your neck. Your arms. Your hands.

Even your tongue is covered with reddish, swelling bumpy things.

But the hives are nothing compared to the feeling of the green goo. It's sliding into your nose, your mouth, even your eyes. It feels like a million snakes, slinking their way into your air passages. You're going to suffocate any second.

All at once, Sam seems to snap out of a trance he's been in. He springs into action — and runs right at Dr. Eeek.

"Have a taste of your own medicine, doctor," Sam yells. Then he smears some of the green gobby goo on the doctor's face.

"Argghhhhhh!" Dr. Eeek screams in terror.

He bolts out of the room. And from the look on his face, you figure he's heading for the antidote!

Follow him to PAGE 80.

"Larry is holding a toothbrush," you tell Dr. Eeek.

"Amazing!" he cries. "You are a true GOOSE-BUMPS expert!"

You grin at Sam. "So how do we get out of the lab now?" you ask eagerly.

"The Canine Maze," Dr. Eeek replies.

"Huh? The Canine Maze?" you repeat. You're sure you must have heard him wrong. "But you said there was another way out if I answered your question right!"

"Too bad. I lied," Dr. Eeek sneers. "It's the Canine Maze for the both of you." Dr. Eeek shivers with delight. He hurries to push a big red button on the wall. A hidden door on the operating room wall swings open.

You and Sam nervously peer inside. You can tell it's a maze because this hallway is much narrower than the regular hall. *Too* narrow, you think. Plus you can't see any doors in the maze. All you can see is that the maze twists and turns a lot.

If you go in, will you ever get out?

Dr. Eeek gestures for you and Sam to enter the maze. "Enjoy yourselves," he says with an evil grin. "Oh, and by the way — *beware of the dogs.*"

Dogs? What dogs? Find out on PAGE 23.

Your throat tightens. Your stomach tightens. The only thing that doesn't tighten is the grip on your wrist.

That's because Dr. Eeek lets go of it. Then he laughs.

"Well, well, well," he chortles. "How do you like it? I've transformed you into a perfect copy of the perfect person — me!"

You feel perfectly sick.

"No!" you shout. "You can't do this!"

But Dr. Eeek isn't listening. He's opening up a closet. He's taking out a raincoat with a big hood. He's putting it on.

It covers his ugly head.

"So long," he says to you. "Sorry to leave you like this, but I've got to go. You see, I've become rather unpopular with the government lately. Too many 'unusual' experiments, they say. So I need to get out of the country. Sorry to say, I'm leaving you here in my place."

Then he runs out of the room. You never see him again.

Oh, well. Who cares? This is only virtual reality, right?

Suddenly the images in your headset stop. You see nothing but black. And the straps loosen on your wrists! You're free!

Or are you?

Find out on PAGE 93.

You stare at the blank screen in your headset. Then slowly, you raise your arms and take the headset off.

Hey — how did your arms get loose? A minute ago they were strapped down in that black chair. Weren't they?

You blink and gaze around the room.

"Welcome back," a smiling face says when your eyes finally focus on the real world.

Mom! She's standing right in front of you — with the police! And Dr. Eeek is still lying on the floor, out cold.

"Mom!" you cry. "How did you get here?"

"You came down to the eighteenth floor and found me," she says. "Remember? And then I called the police and — "

But that was just in the virtual reality game. Wasn't it?

You shake your head and don't say anything. Why bother? You and Sam are safe now. And Dr. Eeek is going to jail. The police tell you they found *all kinds* of creepy stuff in his labs. Including a giant toad that can sing!

"A giant toad that can sing?" Sam asks. A smile creeps across his face. Then he bolts out of the room and dashes down the hall, searching for it.

Uh-oh. Here you go again! Maybe this really isn't . . .

THE END

You decide to wander the maze.

"Woof!" you bark at Sam.

You trot off to explore the maze. Sam follows slowly. Pretty soon you find your way back to the door to the Canine Maze. The one that Dr. Eeek locked, when he put you in the maze.

You lie down and wait. After all, Dr. Eeek has to open that door sometime, doesn't he?

Yup.

It takes a few hours, but he finally opens it.

And you attack! You spring at him, snarling, snapping. You sink your sharp teeth into his ankle. Grrrr! You hate the taste of his pant leg. But you don't care.

You chomp down as if your life depended on it. Which it does.

"Yeooowwwwwch!" Dr. Eeek cries. He staggers backward, trying to shake you off.

But you won't let go! You're vicious! You're an animal.

You're going to hang on to his leg until he gets the message — and turns you back into a human being!

Hang on till you get to PAGE 60.

Your mouth falls open as you stare through the lab window. To your amazement, the lab is filled with chimps! But they're not just monkeying around. They're doing cool things — playing checkers, painting pictures, and reading books.

"Look!" Sam says. "Those two chimps are playing video games! Wow! Can you believe their scores?"

"What kind of research are you doing in here?" you ask Professor Yzark.

"Studying the brains of chimpanzees," he explains. "Chimps are very smart. And physically they're a lot like people. There is much we can learn from them."

Oscar gives the professor a nudge. A *hard* nudge — as if he wants something.

The professor jumps a little. Then he turns to you. "Oscar is wondering if you'd care to go inside," Professor Yzark says. He nods toward the next room. "To see the research . . . up close."

"Sure!" Sam cries. "Can we play video games?"

"Oscar would like that very much," Professor Yzark replies with a strange smile.

What's he smiling about? you wonder.

"Come on!" Sam urges you. "What are you waiting for?"

If you go into the room with the chimps, turn to PAGE 67.

If not, then think of an excuse on PAGE 108.

Dr. Eeek leads you down the hallway. Past a dozen closed doors. Around a corner.

Then all at once, you see it. A hospital operating room. Dr. Eeek pushes open the two swinging doors.

"Huh?" you choke, gulping loudly. "Where are the dogs? Where's the canine lab?"

"This is it," Dr. Eeek replies. He hands you two hospital gowns. "Get changed."

Get changed? Is he kidding? Don't you need your parents' permission for things like this?

"Uh, I've changed my mind," you mumble. "I think I'd better ask my mom about this."

"Too late for that," Dr. Eeek declares.

Then he puts his hands on your shoulders and pushes you through the swinging doors.

Hey! you think. He can't push you around this way!

Push back on PAGE 103.

What was that brown stuff you ate? Whatever it was, it has turned you and Sam into German shepherds.

Dr. Eeek is sneakier than you realized. That food machine was a trick — and you took the bait.

You growl at Sam. He growls back, showing his sharp canine teeth.

Okay, okay, you think. You'll back down. Sam's bigger than you are, anyway.

You glance away from Sam and put your tail between your legs to let him know that he's in charge. He's "top dog."

Then you back out of the way, so that Sam can lick the last scraps of the brown stuff from the floor.

A minute later, the hair on the back of your neck stands up. You smell something — more dogs! You can hear them coming, too. Their sharp nails click on the tile floor.

Big trouble, you think, beginning to panic. You and Sam are trapped in a tiny opening at the end of that narrowing hall.

In a *dead* end.

Think quick! What are you going to do?

If you run out and attack the pack of dogs, turn to PAGE 126.

If you roll over and play dead, turn to PAGE 89.

"Hey — it's a rest room!" you cry.

"Here," Dr. Eeek says, handing you a bucket and a mop. "Clean up."

"Clean up?" you exclaim.

"Correct," Dr. Eeek says. "Floors . . . sinks . . . all of it. I want it all scrubbed and spotless before you leave." Then he marches out of the room.

Clean sinks? He wants you to clean sinks?

Then you and Sam glance around. "Weird," you mutter. "*Look* at those sinks!"

"They're so high!" Sam exclaims. "They're almost eight feet off the ground!"

"I wonder what kind of guy needs a sink that tall?" you ask.

An instant later, the door opens. A *humongous* twelve-foot-tall kid — a kid your age — stomps into the rest room.

"Hi," he says in a booming voice. Then he notices you staring at his height. "Yeah, I know," he groans. "I'm a freak. Dr. Eeek did this to me. But you guys are lucky. You get to clean sinks. Whatever you do, don't do the Raster experiment."

Clean sinks? you think again. Hey — gladly! Any day! And when you're done, you can wash your hands of this whole creepy mess!

THE END

Don't be silly. Of *course* Dr. Eeek is going to come in! This is his office, you goof. He's got the key!

Did you really think you could lock him out of his own office?

You're in big trouble now.

Your only chance is to worm your way out of this.

Go to PAGE 26.

The only speck of light anywhere is the glow-in-the-dark face on Dr. Eeek's wristwatch.

In the darkness, you can feel him bend his head to look at it. He groans.

"What?" you ask.

"Nothing," Dr. Eeek says. "It's just that they're right on time."

"Who?" you ask.

"The electric company," Dr. Eeek says. "I'm afraid I haven't paid my electric bill for the past three months. They threatened to turn off the power at 7:00 P.M. if I didn't come up with the cash. I guess they weren't kidding."

Kidding? Nope — they weren't kidding.

And you're not laughing either. Why? Because it takes a big gulp of air to laugh. And you're out of air in . . .

THE END

"Off!" you yell at the dogs.

You learned that by watching a show on TV about how to train dogs.

Your mom starts laughing. "Oh, dear," she says, chuckling harder every minute. "What on earth are you doing?"

"I'm trying to save your life!" you shriek. "I thought those dogs were — "

Your mom is laughing so hard now that she's crying. But she manages to pull a small silver whistle out of her pocket. She blows it. Instantly the dogs stop barking and run away.

"Those dogs," your mom explains, wiping her eyes, "are part of my research at the lab. Did you really think they'd hurt me?"

Your head is spinning. So much has happened!

"But what about your shoes? What about Dr. Eeek?" you cry.

"Oh, I let the dogs play with my shoes," your mom says. "They like it. And as for Dr. Eeek, I'm sure he tried to scare you. He's just a little crazy. Ignore him."

Ignore him? Is she kidding? He's a lunatic!

But your mom sounds so sincere. You're about to go along with her. And then you see it. The beauty mark.

What's going on? Find out on PAGE 124.

"Let go! Let go!" Dr. Eeek screams.

He shoves his hand into the pocket of his white lab coat and pulls out a silver whistle. He blows it hard.

AAAAAAHHHHH! The sound is killing you! It's so loud. It pierces your ears. You want to yowl and scream. But you don't. You just sink your teeth into his leg. And bite harder.

"Oh, dear," Dr. Eeek moans. "You're not a dog. You're that kid!"

GRRRRRRR-Right! You growl. You hope he gets the point.

"I'll turn you back into a human!" he cries. "Just let me go!"

Hey — you're not that dumb! You don't let go.

With you still attached to his leg, Dr. Eeek limps into a nearby lab room. He opens a white metal drawer and scoops out a red pill. It looks like an M&M — only *much* bigger. It's about the size of a very large grape.

He offers it to you. "Here. Eat this," Dr. Eeek says. "It will turn you back into a person. I think."

He *thinks*? Wait a minute. Does he know what he's doing — or not? Or is this a trick? To swallow the pill, you'll have to let go of his leg. Should you do it?

If you swallow the pill, turn to PAGE 106.

If you won't open your mouth, turn to PAGE 100.

Uh-oh. You're not quite tall enough. No matter how many times you jump and leap and throw yourself into the air, you can't quite reach that button.

Soon, you're dog-tired. You lie down on the floor, panting from exhaustion. You cover your eyes with your paws. You don't even want to look at the world. You know, in your little doggy heart, that you're never going to get out of there. You'll be a dog forever.

But hey — that isn't all bad, is it? There are some good things about being a dog. . . .

Like what?

Like the fact that sooner or later, Dr. Eeek will wander into the maze.

And you've got a big, strong jaw . . . full of long, pointy teeth!

Revenge?

You bet.

Sure, you're a dog. But who said you always have to be man's best friend?

THE END

"It's not that much farther," you say. "Let's keep going."

"Okay," Sam agrees.

"The hall's so narrow, we'd better walk single file," you suggest. "You go first."

"Nah — you first," Sam counters.

"No, really. After you."

How long can you keep this up?

Not long. Finally you pull a coin out of your pocket. You flip it. "Heads, I'll go first. Tails, you go first," you tell Sam.

Flip a coin. If it comes up heads, turn to PAGE 68.

Tails — turn to PAGE 91.

"No way," you tell Vanessa. "We're not here for any experiment. We're waiting for my mom."

Vanessa narrows her eyes at you. Her dark hair cascades over her lab coat. She looks like the witch in *Snow White*.

"Wait here," Vanessa instructs. "I'll get Dr. Eeek."

A moment later, an older man with gray hair walks through the door. Dr. Eeek is wearing a white lab coat just like Vanessa's. But he has his on backward. His face is soft and fleshy, and there's something odd about his right cheek. The flesh looks as if it has been pulled up to meet his right eye — and then stapled there. It gives him a weird squint.

"Well, well," Dr. Eeek begins, squinting at you. He sounds like a school principal who's just caught you stealing candy from the snack machine. "What can I do for you two?"

"I'm just waiting for my mom," you announce firmly.

He asks your name, and you tell him.

"Ah, yes," Dr. Eeek says. "Follow me."

Follow him over to PAGE 41.

Dr. Eeek is too weird, you decide. You start to back out of the room. But Sam still has dollar signs in his eyes.

"Where are you going?" Sam whispers to you.

"Out of here," you declare.

"No way," he insists. "I'm staying until I get the money."

Dr. Eeek grins. He can tell you are having second thoughts.

"How bad can it be?" Sam mutters under his breath. "I mean seriously. Your mom *works* here. It's got to be a safe place — right?"

You nod half-heartedly.

But where is your mom, anyway?

As if he can read your mind, Dr. Eeek speaks up. "Actually," he says, "I'm not sure you're right for the Raster experiment. I think you two are more suited to something . . ."

He lets his voice trail off.

". . . else," he finally says.

This sounds worse every minute!

If you do whatever Dr. Eeek tells you to do, turn to PAGE 25.

If you chicken out, turn to PAGE 17.

You quickly roll the receptionist's swivel chair across the room. You plant it behind the door, so you'll be in position to ambush whoever's coming. Then you search around for a weapon.

There must be *something* you can use to conk the person on the head!

"How about this?" Sam asks, handing you the telephone.

"Hey — good idea!" you say. You hold the phone over your head like a club and wait. You stand on the swivel chair.

The door opens, and Vanessa walks in.

You lunge forward with the phone. You reach out, trying to smack her with it.

But suddenly the swivel chair swivels, then slides.

Whoops . . . the wheels are rolling . . . rolling . . . you're losing your balance . . . and . . .

BAM!

The chair rolls out from under you.

You fly forward and hit the floor.

A moment later, everything goes black.

Go to PAGE 69.

You blow the silver whistle again. Harder this time.

But still, no sound comes out.

What's wrong with this thing? you want to shout. But your voice is paralyzed — with fear.

You blow one more time. Still no sound. But just then you notice something. The dogs are backing down! All six of them. They stop barking. Stop lunging at you. And all six of them *sit*! They just sit down on their back haunches and stare up at you, as if they're waiting for further instructions.

"Cool!" Sam exclaims. "That must be a dog whistle. You know — they make a high-pitched sound. People can't hear it, but dogs can. Where did you get it?"

"It's a long story. I'll tell you later," you say, wiping the sweat off your brow. "Come on — let's find a way out of this place."

Look for the exit on PAGE 97.

Why not take a quick look around the lab? you think.

After all — your mom never lets you do anything like this. She never shows you *any* of this cool stuff. This might be your only chance.

"Yeah — we'd love to see the chimps," you tell Professor Yzark.

Professor Yzark smiles. Oscar jumps up and down.

"Good," Professor Yzark says. Quickly he ushers you and Sam through the connecting door.

As soon as you walk in, all the chimps glance up. They stare at you and Sam without making a sound.

Weird, you think.

You hold very still, not wanting to scare the chimps. That's why you don't notice what's happening behind you.

Oscar the chimp is slamming the door . . .

And locking it with a key!

Hey! What's going on?

Find out on PAGE 10.

68

The coin comes up heads.

You gulp and squeeze past Sam, so you can lead the way.

One step at a time, you creep to the end of the corridor.

The walls get narrower . . . narrower. . . . In fact, they're only about a foot apart now. You can hardly squeeze through.

But now that you're almost to the end, you notice something. The walls don't come to a point. The corridor is just super-narrow for about fifteen feet. And then there's an opening!

You turn sideways, suck in your stomach, and edge your way to the end of the hall.

To the opening. And then you see it!

Go on to PAGE 72.

You wake up in the waiting room. Vanessa is towering over you. And Sam is crouching beside you.

"Are you okay?" Sam asks.

Before you can answer, Vanessa reaches into her lab coat and pulls out a spray can. There's a sign on it in big red letters. It reads:

SLEEPING SPRAY — THE DEADLY DUST
OF NIGHTFALL

She points the can in your direction and *Pssssss!* — she sprays it in your face. Then in Sam's.

Then she starts to sing. "Lullaby . . . and good night . . ."

You glance over at Sam. He has slumped to the floor. His eyes are closing. So are yours. But before you fall into a deep, deep sleep, you hear him speak his last words.

"The phone . . . I mean you should use it to call 911," he says.

Oh, yeah. That would have been a good idea!

Well, maybe next time.

But this time, you're going to lullaby land — and they don't have any phones there. Just a great big sign, with big red letters on it saying . . .

THE END

You call Dominick's Pizza.

"Hello, may I take your order please?" the voice on the other end of the line says.

"Help! You've got to help me!" you scream into the phone. "I'm trapped in Eeek Labs and — "

"Eeek Labs? Okay, so you want your usual — a large half-mushroom, half-pepperoni. It'll be right there."

"No, wait!" you scream. "I'm trapped here! You've got to come get me out!"

"Hey — is this a prank?" the guy at the pizza place says.

"No! It's not a prank! I'm locked in with Dr. Eeek, and he's doing something terrible to my friend, and — "

The line goes dead.

Hurry to PAGE 39.

You can't believe it!

Your clothes are torn! Your arms and legs are scratched and bleeding from the thorns in the prickly bushes!

"How — ? What happened?" you cry. "I thought that was just virtual reality."

Dr. Eeek gives you a nasty smile. "Never mind," he grumbles. "Your part of the experiment is over. You are free to go — if you really want to. Or . . ."

Or *what*? Is he nuts? Of course you want to leave!

Until you gaze over at Sam. He's still strapped into his black leather chair with his headset on — and he's clutching his throat. He starts to scream.

"Help!" Sam cries. "Please — someone! Help!"

"As I said, you may leave," Dr. Eeek says. "Or you can return to the virtual reality — *Sam's* reality — and try to save him." Dr. Eeek snickers. "Without you, I'm afraid he's not going to make it."

Oh, no! You've got to do something to help your friend! But what?

If you're willing to put on the headset, turn to PAGE 105.

If you run out of there and try to find someone to help Sam, turn to PAGE 84.

"What is it? What's in that room?" Sam demands.

A slow grin spreads across your face.

"Is it a way out?" Sam asks eagerly.

"Nope." You shake your head. "But it's something almost as good."

"What?" Sam asks, sounding almost grouchy.

"Vending machines!" you shout. You whirl around to give Sam a high five.

"Yes!" he says, squeezing through the narrow hall and into the opening with you.

You didn't notice it before, but you're starving. Your stomach has been growling for half an hour.

You check out the machines. They're the kind with a glass globe full of candy or bubble gum. But instead of candy, they have some kind of brown crumbly stuff in them. Maybe it's nuts, or something like granola.

"Oh, no," you say. "Health food."

"Who cares?" Sam cries. "I'm starving."

True. You *are* starving. And besides, the machines don't have coin slots. Could all this stuff be free?

Find out on PAGE 83.

"You slime!" you shout at Dr. Eeek.

His eyes are still closed, so he doesn't see you coming. You leap at him with your goo-covered hands. You smear the goo on his chin, mouth, and eyebrows.

"Ha, ha, ha!" Dr. Eeek shouts, tossing his head back and roaring with laughter.

What's so funny? you wonder.

And then it hits you — haven't you been through all of this before?

That's when you see him reach behind his ear — and peel off another mask!

Oh, no, you realize. He may be crazy — but he's also very smart.

Smarter than you.

Now what are you going to do, hotshot?

Never mind — it doesn't matter *what* you do because Dr. Eeek will always have another mask underneath the first. You can't slime him. You can't escape him. And guess what else?

Your twenty seconds are up!

Say "Gooo-bye." Because this is . . .

THE END

Are you kidding? You're going to hide under the operating table?

Think again. The sheet that's draped over the half-boy, half-dog will only half cover you.

Which means that this was only a half-baked plan.

Dr. Eeek hurries in and spots you immediately.

"Ah-ha!" he exclaims. He leers at you and rubs his hands. "I see you've decided to stay a little longer — and cooperate."

Before you can scramble away, Dr. Eeek grabs you. He forces you to drink a foaming purple liquid. Then he hooks you up to some machines . . . and in half an hour, he's turned you into half-kid, half-dog, half-basketball!

Hey — that's too many halves!

But try telling that to Dr. Eeek. *He* doesn't care.

You look in the mirror and shriek. The basketball half is attached where you used to have a head!

If you have half a brain, you'll make better choices next time.

But then, you probably don't have half a brain anymore — do you?

THE END

You freeze. You hold perfectly, completely still. You don't even breathe. You don't want to attract too much attention.

How *nice* of you! The Komodo dragon really appreciates your cooperation.

CHOMP!

He doesn't even have to use his tail to knock you to the ground. He just digs his razor-sharp teeth into your side and . . . let's just say you make a tasty snack.

What's wrong? You didn't expect it to end this way? You thought this was just virtual reality? You thought it was just a game?

Sorry. It might be virtual reality — but it's the only reality you've got right now!

And if it's just a game, YOU LOSE!

GAME OVER

"You'll never get out of the lab . . . unless you can find your way out of the Canine Maze!" Dr. Eeek warns.

He pulls at his lab coat to adjust it. It's practically choking him, since he's wearing it backward. But he doesn't seem to think there is anything wrong.

He strokes his chin, thinking. You are pretty sure from the look on Dr. Eeek's face that he's cooking up a hideous plot. Then he nods.

"Yes — I'd say that's your best chance," Dr. Eeek declares. "The Canine Maze. Unless . . ."

"Unless what?" you cry.

"Unless you know the answer to this special GOOSEBUMPS question," Dr. Eeek replies.

"Excellent!" you shout. "I'm a GOOSEBUMPS expert." You slap Sam a high five.

"Okay," Dr. Eeek begins, "in the book *My Hairiest Adventure*, when Larry first notices the thick black hair growing on his hands, what is he holding? A toothbrush or a hairbrush?"

If you think it's a toothbrush, turn to PAGE 49.

If you choose a hairbrush, turn to PAGE 116.

"No way!" you shout at Dr. Eeek. "I'm not going to be your guinea pig!"

Then, with the goo growing all over your face, you turn and bolt for the door.

"Come on, Sam! Let's run!" you try to say.

The two of you sprint like world-class athletes, down the hall to the waiting room. And luckily, that big vault door in front is standing slightly ajar. So you zoom into the hall and catch a down elevator.

"Ewwww — yuk!" a teenage girl in the elevator cries when she sees you.

Uh-oh. The green stuff. It's grossing her out.

"I don't know what she's complaining about," Sam says. "I mean, look at her. Her skin is green!"

Yeah, you think to yourself. And so is her hair . . . and her clothes . . . and . . .

Hey, hold on. Everything looks green to you!

Then you catch a glimpse of yourself in a highly polished chrome elevator panel. That's when you realize — the goo has completely covered your head!

Take another look at yourself on PAGE 33.

"Don't even turn around," you whisper to Sam. "Just keep on walking."

The two of you hurry down the hall. Past the many lab doors. Heading straight toward the reception area.

"My mom will probably be waiting for us," you assure Sam.

"Yeah," Sam replies. "And then we can get out of this creepy place."

"You've got it," you say, trying to convince yourself.

But what if she's not?

You pull open the door to the waiting room — and gasp!

There's a snarling, growling German shepherd standing there — blocking the only exit!

And he has something you recognize in his mouth!

Hurry to PAGE 115.

"Help!" you scream at the top of your lungs.

But why scream? you ask yourself.

Dr. Eeek isn't going to come help you. And Sam can't. He's strapped into that black chair. And that vault door is supposed to be "locked at all times." The receptionist said so.

So who do you think is going to open it and rescue you?

The pizza delivery guy, of course!

An instant later, the front door opens — and the Dominick's Pizza guy walks in.

"Hi," he says, as the water gushes out into the hallway, soaking his legs. "Here's the pizza you ordered. Half-mush, half-pep. Right?"

You stare at him, open-mouthed. He doesn't even seem to mind that he's getting wet.

"How did you get in here?" you ask him, dumbfounded.

He holds up a key, dangling from a long chain. "Dr. Eeek orders almost every day," he explains. "So we've got a key. We just let ourselves in and leave the pizza. We send him a bill every month. This is what you wanted, right?"

You shake your head. This is unbelievable!

Believe it on PAGE 120.

You follow Dr. Eeek as he races down the hall, pulls open another lab door, and hurries in.

Inside, there is an enormous glass box with a hinged door. Dr. Eeek dashes into the chamber and tries to pull the door closed.

"Not so fast!" you shout. You and Sam dash into the box with him.

It's like cramming three sweaty people into a phone booth. Too close for comfort. And you can tell there is very little air inside.

But who cares? The minute Dr. Eeek closes the door, a white gas fills the box — and the goo dissolves!

You were right! It's the antidote box! You're saved!

Except . . .

"How come this door won't open?" Sam asks. He bangs on the handle.

"Hey — how come the lights just went out?" you cry.

You stare into the total pitch-darkness of the lab.

You're locked in an airtight box with a crazy person!

Turn to PAGE 58.

"Sam!" you call. You rush back to the room where you left him — the one with three locks.

Luckily they aren't locked. You yank open the door.

Sam sits blindfolded at a table inside the small, empty room. He holds a spoon in his hand.

In front of him are three bowls of cereal.

Dr. Eeek stands behind Sam with a clipboard and a pencil.

"Which one tastes like sugar-coated Ping-Pong balls?" Dr. Eeek asks. "Which one tastes like cinnamon potato chips? Which one tastes like moldy hay?"

Huh? A taste test?

That's *all*?

You smack your forehead. What a jerk you've been. And Sam's going to get fifty dollars for this!

"Uh, Dr. Eeek," you say. "Is it too late to change my mind? I'd like to do this experiment, too."

Dr. Eeek laughs. "I'm sorry," he says. "This experiment is over. But I'd be happy to use you both in my canine lab."

Canine lab? What sort of experiments is he doing with dogs?

Turn to PAGE 111.

Quickly you try to pull the sticky, glowing green stuff off Sam's hands. But it's *really* stuck! You can get only about half of it off.

And guess what?

Now your hands are stuck together, too!

"Have fun, people," Dr. Eeek says. He salutes you briskly, with a quick snap of his hand over that weird eye. Then he shuffles out of the room.

For the next few minutes, you and Sam struggle with the goo. You claw at your hands and your arms, trying to pull it off. But it's no use. The stuff is too sticky.

And it's growing thicker all the time.

Within minutes, the goo has grown all the way up both of your arms — and it's starting to encircle your throat!

Just as it slides toward your mouth, Dr. Eeek returns.

"Well, people, how are we doing?" he says with an evil smile. "Are we ready to cooperate now? Because I can get that stuff off you — if you're willing to do the Raster experiment."

If you cooperate with Dr. Eeek, turn to PAGE 9.

If you smear some of the goo on Dr. Eeek, turn to PAGE 37.

If you just RUN LIKE MAD! — turn to PAGE 77.

Sam twists a knob. A handful of the brown stuff tumbles down the chute. It *is* free!

"What is it?" you ask, peering closely at the food in Sam's hand.

"Who cares?" Sam replies. He pops some of it into his mouth and starts to chew. "I think it's granola."

Slowly you turn the crank on the vending machine. You put a few pieces of the stuff in your mouth. At first, it just tastes sort of salty. But then . . .

"Yuk!" you yell, spitting it out on the floor.

If you didn't know better, you'd think this stuff was dog food!

"Take another bite," Sam says. "It's good, once you get used to it."

Sam keeps turning the crank and eating the granola. He stuffs all his pockets with the brown crunchy food. It's Sam's policy never, ever to turn down *anything* that's free.

How about you? Do you want to take another bite — or not?

If yes, turn to PAGE 107.
If no, turn to PAGE 94.

No way are you going to let Dr. Eeek strap you in that chair again.

"I'm free to go? Then I'm outta here," you say, waving good-bye and walking out of the room casually.

As soon as you're out of the room, you break into a run. Feet pounding, you race down the hall toward the empty reception area. Dash to the door and . . .

But wait a minute. That thick steel vault door is locked — and you can't get out!

Quickly you pick up the phone on the receptionist's desk. You dial your mom's phone number at work.

Wherever she is — maybe she'll answer the phone.

Ring . . . ring . . . ring . . . ring . . . ring . . .

You let it ring ten times, but there's no answer.

Oh, no. You've got to do something to save Sam — quick!

Your hands are sweaty. Your heart is beating in your throat. You can't think of anything to do.

So you call the one other phone number you've memorized.

Turn to PAGE 70.

You bend over, lowering your arms — er, uh, front legs! — to the floor.

Front legs? Yikes! You glance down and your heart almost stops. Your arms have fur on them!

Your tongue hangs out, and you begin to pant. And sniff.

You sniff the floor. You sniff Sam's front legs.

Sam's front legs? Yikes, again!

Oh, no, you slowly realize. You and Sam have turned into dogs!

Be a good dog and turn to PAGE 55.

No way you're sticking around with a Komodo dragon — you RUN! You dash into the bushes and sprint like crazy. But the bushes are filled with prickly thorns.

The Komodo dragon is on your tail — sort of. You don't really have a tail — he does. But he's chasing you.

You trip, and he manages to sink his big, jagged teeth into your shoe!

You stumble to your feet and run in a zigzag pattern. You read somewhere that Komodo dragons can't make quick turns. You hope this will help you escape.

You're right. The Komodo dragon gives up. It's fast — but it can't hang in there very long. It stops chasing you and turns around to go the other way. Finally you drop to the ground, dead tired.

Dr. Eeek takes the headset off you. "The experiment is over," he announces. But when you glance down at your arms and legs, you scream!

Find out why on PAGE 71.

"Uh, this is too weird," you tell Sam. "I'm going back."

You turn around and retrace your steps. Back to the place where you could have turned left.

Ahhhh — this is more like it. At least the hallway isn't making you feel all-closed-in now. You take the left fork.

Dog smell.

Then you turn right.

More dog smell.

"This place is freaky," you whisper to Sam. "I can smell dogs all around me. But it's so quiet. Where are they?"

Where are they?

Before Sam can answer, you find out. All at once — as if they've been released from a pen somewhere — you hear dogs racing toward you, barking savagely!

Barking in front of you. Barking behind you.

"We've got to get out of here!" Sam shouts. "There's another left turn up ahead."

"We *can't* get out," you shriek. "They're coming from every direction!"

Sam doesn't have time to answer. Because at that instant, the dogs arrive!

Hurry to PAGE 18.

You pull your left hand back and make a fist. Then you wind up and throw the punch of a lifetime.

POW!

It decks Dr. Eeek, easy. He's out cold.

Then you and Sam run at top speed. Out of the lab. Down the hall. To the waiting room. When you get there, the big vault door is standing open.

Your heart pounds. Sweat drips from your hair. You can hardly believe you've finally escaped that madman!

You dash into the hall and hammer on the elevator button. You think if you press it more times, it'll arrive sooner.

Finally the elevator comes, and you and Sam step in.

You press the button for the eighteenth floor — one floor below. That's where your mom's office is, right?

The elevator goes down one floor. But when the door opens on eighteen, you gasp.

You are staring into *nothing.*

Not a room. Not a hallway. Just empty space. Utter nothingness!

Turn to PAGE 90.

You decide to play it safe. You cower in the corner by the dog food machine, waiting. Lying still.

Pretty soon, you hear them coming. Six blood-thirsty German shepherds. Running. Barking. Barking. Running. More barking.

The sound fills the small corridor and hurts your ears — which are more sensitive now that you're a dog.

Finally the dogs race into the small opening where you and Sam are hiding.

You don't move. You just lie there, pretending to be asleep.

German shepherds aren't going to attack one of their own kind, are they?

Unfortunately, you may think you're a dog, but the dogs don't. They can smell your human blood — and they've been trained to attack!

Remember how you decided to roll over and play dead? Well, bad news. You're not pretending anymore.

THE END

"What is this?" Sam asks. You both peer into the emptiness in front of you.

You think quickly. It looks like the blank screen you saw before Dr. Eeek turned on the virtual reality machine.

Then you get it. "It's nothing," you tell Sam. "Because Dr. Eeek didn't program it! He didn't program the eighteenth floor — or my mom — or anything else in this building."

"Oh, no," Sam moans. "Then we're stuck?"

Go to PAGE 8.

The coin comes up tails.

Okay, you think. Sam can lead the way down the narrowing hallway. That will give you a chance to look around.

You start to examine the floor. The walls. The ceiling. Maybe there's another way out of this place. . . .

Hey — what's that crack in the wall?

You stare to your left and see what looks like a sliding panel. You press on it. It slides open. You stop, frozen. You peer into the passageway. What *is* that in the darkness?

"Sam! Hey, Sam!" you whisper. "There's something here!"

"Huh?" Sam whirls around and stares into the dark, too.

A large shape looms in the blackness.

"Sh-should we check it out?" you stutter.

Sam squints, trying to see what's ahead. Nothing moves. "Sure," Sam replies, with a shrug. "Let's go. It's probably just a shadow."

You and Sam inch into the passageway.

And then you realize that Sam was wrong. That thing is *not* a shadow.

You hold back a scream. You grab Sam's arm and point.

To see what awaits you in the darkness, turn to PAGE 121.

Congratulations. You leap into the air and BINGO! You hit the button with your nose!

All at once, a piece of the wall slides open, revealing a stairwell. You and Sam run in. You sniff. Something smells familiar.

Sniff-sniff-sniff.

What *is* that smell?

And then you realize. It's your mom's perfume!

You follow the scent, down the stairs to the floor below. To a door that is closed. You bark until someone comes to open it. Who is it?

"Mom!" you try to cry when you see her. You jump up on her, barking and wagging your tail.

"Get down," she scolds. "What are you dogs doing in here, anyway?"

Then she turns and calls to someone behind her. "Hey, Harold, come here and look. A pair of dogs! They probably escaped from Eeek's lab."

"Mom, don't you recognize me?" you want to ask. But all you are able to say is, "Woof. Woof-woof-woof. Woof."

Go on to PAGE 118.

You tear off the headset and jump out of the black leather chair.

"Sam!" you shout. "Let's get out of this place!"

Sam glares at you, his eyes full of hate.

"What did you do with my friend?" he cries.

"Sam! It's me!" you shout. "I *am* your friend! I just don't look like myself. Dr. Eeek turned me into a copy of him."

Sam shakes his head and backs away from you as fast as he can. You run after him. But for some reason he's much faster than you. He reaches the waiting room first, then dials 911. He stands on the desk so you can't reach him while he talks on the phone.

Why can't you reach him? Because no matter how hard you try, you can't seem to climb up on the desk. Your legs hurt too much. You have creaky old joints — caused by arthritis!

Arthritis? That old person's disease? Of course! You're Dr. Eeek — a fifty-eight-year-old man! Bad luck. You've got bad breath and a bad back, too.

Before you know it, the police are on their way. They arrest you for doing experiments on kids. And when Sam tells them that *you* are missing, they throw you in jail for kidnapping, too — and throw away the key.

THE END

"No thanks," you say, making a face.

That brown crunchy stuff tastes gross!

You turn your back on Sam and take a peek around the corner, into the hall, to see if anyone's coming. After all — you *are* in a canine maze. And Dr. Eeek *did* say beware of the dogs.

And besides — it gives you the creeps to be here. Trapped in a tiny room at the end of a skinny hall.

Then you smell it again. Dog smell. But stronger. And really, really close.

You hear a growl. Behind you! Your muscles tighten. You whirl again — just in time to see Sam transforming into a dog!

"No!" you cry out. You watch as his canine teeth grow longer! Then the hair. The short brown hair. It pops out all over his arms. Or really, his legs. His *four* legs.

"Sam! Stop eating that stuff!" you scream.

But it's too late. In the next instant, the transformation is complete. Sam's a German shepherd — and he's ready to attack!

Well, Dr. Eeek told you to beware of the dogs. Too bad he didn't tell you to beware of your best friend!

THE END

"This way!" you shout to Sam. You turn left and run down the long white hallway.

In a minute, you reach a door at the end. You yank it open.

BINGO!

You're back in the waiting room!

"We did it!" Sam yells, slapping you a high five. "Let's get out of here!"

But just as you're about to race to the front door, you freeze. It's that vault door — the one that's six inches thick. Only there's one big problem.

There's no handle on the *inside*. No doorknob. Nothing. No way to open it.

"Maybe it pushes open," you say. You race across the room and lunge at it. *Ouch!* You ram your shoulder into the door, but it doesn't budge.

"We're trapped," Sam moans. "We're locked in!"

Oh, no, you think. And then you hear footsteps! Someone's coming. Probably Dr. Eeek. What now?

Maybe you'd better hide behind the door — and ambush whoever comes in.

Hide on PAGE 65.

The blob of green goo flies toward you. Sam dives in front of you and catches it. It's an old habit of his. Hogging the ball.

Dr. Eeek chuckles. "Nice catch," he declares in a deep, sinister voice. "How do you like my new invention?"

Sam stares down at his hands. His eyebrows wrinkle with worry. The green goo is sticking to his hands — and he can't seem to get them apart!

"What *is* this stuff?" Sam moans.

"That's one of my very best experimental results," Dr. Eeek replies. "I call it my G-substance. G for green. G for glowing. G for gooey."

"How about G for '*Get* it off me!' " Sam shrieks.

You gasp. The stuff seems to be growing up Sam's arm!

"Ah, yes," Dr. Eeek says. "And I forgot to mention. G for *growing*, too."

"Help!" Sam screams. The goo slowly creeps up both of his arms, toward his face.

Quick! Help your best friend on PAGE 82.

It takes about twenty minutes, but you and Sam finally do escape. You find an emergency exit door in the Canine Maze. It leads into a stairwell that leads to the floor below, which is where your mom's lab has been all the time.

You hurry into her office. She's bent over a microscope, lost in her work.

"Oh, hi!" your mom says, looking at her watch. "I guess I forgot the time. Ready for a movie? I thought we'd go see the new science fiction film about the crazy scientist who traps these two kids and — "

You and Sam glance at each other and roll your eyes.

"Hold it, Mom," you interrupt. "Sam and I were thinking. We'd rather do something . . . uh . . . a little less exciting. Could we just go home, eat pizza, watch cartoons, and then go to bed?"

Your mom stares at you blankly.

"Uh, okay," she replies. "But I hate to think you came all the way to my lab for nothing. Isn't there something fun we could do? How about if we stop on the way home and get a scary book to read?"

You and Sam roll your eyes again. A scary book? Now?

"Not tonight, Mom," you tell her. "Not tonight!"

THE END

"Sure," you insist. "Anything."

Dr. Eeek doesn't even chuckle. He straight-out laughs. A big, roaring, throwing-his-head-back-and-laughing-in-your-face laugh.

"Great!" he cries, rubbing his hands together.

Sam stares at you and just shakes his head.

"Not me," Sam says. "I'll stay here and take my chance with the doggy thing."

You wave good-bye to Sam. Dr. Eeek leads you down the hall and around the corner to a pink door. Then he opens it. And pushes you into a room full of feathers. White feathers. Brown feathers. Pink flamingo feathers.

They're piled so deep, they come up to your waist.

It tickles your ankles to move through this big mass of fluff. But otherwise it feels sort of soft and nice.

"Take off your shoes," Dr. Eeek orders you, still laughing.

Get barefoot on PAGE 109.

Sam's all right, you decide. And besides — that cry definitely came from somewhere in *front* of you.

"Help! Please!" the voice calls out desperately.

It seems to be coming from a room just a few feet ahead.

You dash forward and pull open a lab door. There's nothing inside except an empty laboratory. A big blob of some kind of green stuff sits on the counter.

Wrong room, you say to yourself.

You continue down the hall. You try another door. Nope. Just a broom closet.

The next door on the left has to be it. It's already partly open. You give it a push — and gasp!

Catch your breath on PAGE 38.

100

No way, you decide. You won't open your mouth.

Wait a minute. Are you kidding? You're *never* going to open your mouth? You're just going to cling to Dr. Eeek's leg for the rest of your life?

Don't be silly. You'll never get out of here that way.

In fact, you've got to open your mouth sooner or later — or you'll starve!

So you might as well start by eating that big red pill.

How bad can it be?

Go to PAGE 106 — and take your medicine.

You follow the chimp. He leads you quickly down the gleaming-white hallway. Oddly enough, he seems to know *exactly* where he's going.

When the chimp's not watching, Sam stoops over. He copies the chimp's lumbering scamper. "Ooo! Ooo!" Sam cries, scratching his underarms and making chimp faces.

The chimp turns around and catches Sam at it. He glares at both of you.

Weird, you think. You know chimps are supposed to be smart animals, but the gleam in this one's eyes . . . ! Frankly, you think, he looks smarter than Sam!

At last you come to a door. The chimp opens it and makes a sound. It sounds kind of like "eeek."

What's in here? you wonder. You step through the door into a large laboratory. Sam follows right behind.

Inside, a tall man wearing a lab coat writes on a clipboard. He whirls around. He glares at you with intense dark eyes.

"Who are you?" he demands loudly. "What are you doing here?"

Explain who you are on PAGE 122.

102

You dash to the right, feet pounding.

"Run — *this* way!" you scream at Sam, who seems to have headed in the opposite direction.

You reach the end of the hallway. You yank open the door to the waiting room.

Uh-oh.

This isn't the waiting room — although there is definitely something *waiting* for you there!

Inside a big steel-walled room sits a huge, horrifying creature with long pointy fangs.

Have you ever seen a cross between a gorilla and a vampire bat?

Well, now you have!

And *cross* is the right word, too. The "vamporilla" thing is so grouchy, it decides to tear you apart just for the exercise.

Cross your fingers that next time you won't cross paths with *this* guy!

And cross yourself off the list of the living, because this is definitely . . .

THE END

"Get your hands off me!" you shout at Dr. Eeek.

But he doesn't back up. You reach out and give him a shove. Then you shove him again. Harder.

"You can't experiment on *kids* like this!" you yell. You give him another push.

He stumbles backwards, slightly dazed, and cowers against a tiled wall.

Then you and Sam charge out through the swinging doors.

You're getting outta this joint!

"Wait. Who are you?" Dr. Eeek calls. "How did you get into my lab, anyway?"

It won't hurt to answer him — will it?

If you think it's safe to answer Dr. Eeek, turn to PAGE 125.

Or maybe you'd better just get out of there on PAGE 78.

Hey — let's face it.

You tried to worm your way out of things, but you just weren't wormy enough in . . .

THE END

You gulp and bravely sit back down in the leather chair. If this is the only way to save Sam, you're willing to do it.

Dr. Eeek straps on the headset — and straps down your arms. Then he pushes some buttons on the console. Instantly you see what Sam is seeing.

YIKES!

Sam is underwater in a huge tank in Eeek Labs — and he's struggling with a two-headed octopus! And if it has two heads, you know without even counting that it must have *sixteen* arms!

You lean over the edge of the tank. You try to give Sam a hand. But before you reach Sam, the octopus reaches out to you!

It wraps one long gray-black tentacle around your neck!

Quick! Save your own neck on PAGE 27.

Slowly, you open your mouth just wide enough to let go of Dr. Eeek's leg. Then you quickly gobble down the red pill in his hand.

Yuk! It tastes terrible.

But almost at once, you can feel yourself changing back into a human being!

You stand up on your back legs and stretch. Ahhh . . . that feels much better. You were getting pretty tired of walking on all fours.

You stare down at your paws. They're changing back into hands and feet. Within a few minutes, you are yourself again.

Phew! Close one!

"Okay," you say to Dr. Eeek. "Here are your choices. Either you go with me to the police — right now — and confess that you've been doing deadly experiments. Or I'll sic my dog on you."

"Your dog?" Dr. Eeek sneers with a nasty laugh.

Then he glances down and sees Sam — who is still a dog! Sam wags his tail at you. He bares his teeth and snarls at Dr. Eeek.

"Don't I have any other choices?" Dr. Eeek asks meekly.

"Not this time," you tell him. "Not this time!"

THE END

You take another bite of the crunchy brown stuff. And then another. Sam's right — it's not so bad. In fact, you eat so much, you begin to feel really full. Or not full, exactly. Top heavy. Like you can't stand up.

All of a sudden, you have an overwhelming urge to drop down to the floor on all fours.

All fours? Wait a minute. You don't *have* four legs.

Do you?

Quick! Find out on PAGE 85.

"Thanks, but we can't go in the lab," you say politely.

"That's okay," Professor Yzark replies. "You probably don't have time anyway. Your mother just telephoned me. She had to go to a meeting. But she wants you to take Oscar home with you. Then someone will drop by your house later today to pick him up."

"Really?" you ask. "Take the chimp home?"

"Cool!" Sam shouts.

But it's not cool. It's not cool at all. The minute you get home, Oscar goes wild. He runs to the refrigerator and helps himself to snacks — but not to eat. To play with! He throws a handful of pineapple yogurt at the wall. Then he starts swinging from the chandeliers.

Help! You and Sam are worn out from chasing Oscar!

"I wish someone would come get this monkey," you say.

That instant, the doorbell rings. You peek out the window. There's a Jeep parked outside. And standing on your porch is a tall, muscular teenager wearing sandals and a pair of cutoff jeans. No shirt. His sun-streaked brown hair hangs down onto his broad, tanned chest. He looks a little familiar — but you can't remember from where.

Who is he?

Answer the door on PAGE 15.

You quickly take off your shoes.

Why not? Even if you *are* incredibly ticklish, this can't be any worse than the Canine Maze.

Can it?

"Heh-heh-heh," you giggle, as you walk barefoot on the tickly feathers.

An instant later, Dr. Eeek dashes out into the hall. He locks the door behind him. You're locked inside!

Then, all at once, a sliding panel in the wall opens. Forty small chimpanzees run into the room. They pick up the feathers and begin tickling you. Behind the ears. On the neck. Under your chin.

And on your feet. The soles of your feet. That's the worst part.

In fact, they tickle you to death.

But at least it's a happy ending, because your last words are "Ha-hah-ah-ha-ha!" — and you end up with a smile on your face!

THE END

110

No whistle?

Oooohhhhh — too bad.

You seemed like such a nice person, too.

But with all six dogs surrounding you, there's no possible way you're going to get out of there.

Not because the dogs attack you, though. They don't. They're trained to simply corner you — and keep you there *forever*.

And forever is a very, very long time, which is why this is

THE END

"I don't know," you say, hesitating. "The canine lab?"

"Don't be a jerk!" Sam exclaims. "Maybe we can get another fifty bucks. And anyway, I love dogs."

You think about it. So far, exploring your mom's lab has been fun. A little scary, but fun. Anyway it's more fun than waiting in the reception area for your mom.

But where *is* your mom?

And what about that person who was calling for help?

Doesn't that worry you?

It does — but you decide to put it out of your mind. It was probably nothing, right? Maybe it wasn't even a real person. Maybe it was just a voice on the radio somewhere. Or on TV.

"Okay," you announce. "I'm in. Let's go to the canine lab."

Dr. Eeek smiles. "Gooood," he says, drawing out the word. "I *knew* you'd cooperate."

He gives you a wink with that weird eye. The one that seems to be stapled to his cheek. It makes him look as if he's permanently squinting.

"Follow me," Dr. Eeek commands.

Head over to the canine lab on PAGE 54.

112

You dash out into the hall, with the whistle in your hand.

Now what?

You can't just leave this place without Sam. . . .

Sam! He's with Dr. Eeek — in a lab down the hall! He's probably in big trouble!

You race back to the room where you left Sam and Dr. Eeek. But it's empty. All you find is a chewing gum wrapper for cinnamon gum. The kind Sam always chews.

Then you notice — there's another part of a gum wrapper on the floor by the door. And another out in the hall. And another.

It's a trail! Sam's trying to tell you where he went!

You follow the gum wrapper trail. Down the hall. Around the corner. And straight into another operating room!

There you find Sam lying on one stainless steel table. And a jar of pickles lying on another.

Electrical wires run from a scary-looking machine to Sam's feet. *And* to the jar of pickles!

"What are you doing!" you scream at Dr. Eeek.

Quick! Turn to PAGE 5.

"No way," you say, eyeing the straps on the two black chairs. "Come on, Sam. Run!"

Without waiting another second, you and Sam bolt for the door. You race back into the lab with the goo. Then out the door and into the hallway. Now . . .

Hey, wait a minute. Which way is the waiting room? Left or right?

Can you remember?

You'd better think fast, because Dr. Eeek is on his way!

If you think the waiting room is to the right, go to PAGE 102.

If you turn left, go to PAGE 95.

114

In a panic, you try to remember what you know about those sprinklers.

Oh, yeah. They're heat sensitive. Your mom told you about them once. When they get hot, the water comes on.

You grab a chair as fast as you can. Then you unplug a table lamp from the receptionist's desk and remove the lamp shade.

This will work, you tell yourself. Won't it?

You stand on the chair, under one of the sprinklers. With the lamp in your hands, you touch the still-hot bulb to the sprinkler head.

For a moment, nothing happens.

Hurry up, you pray silently. Is this thing going to work or not?

Turn to PAGE 19.

"That's my mom's shoe!" you cry, pointing at the blue-and-green thing in the German shepherd's mouth.

The dog growls again when you point. His teeth are dripping with drool. And the look in his eyes is killer. Pure killer.

"Huh?" Sam says. "How do you know?"

"Because I know," you manage to choke out. "I recognize it. No one else has shoes like my mom's."

Sam gulps loudly at your side. For some reason, he can't take his eyes off the dog. And the dog won't take his eyes off Sam. The two of them are having a stare-down.

"Where did he come from?" Sam asks nervously.

"Probably from Dr. Eeek's canine lab," you reply.

And then it hits you. Your mom could be there, too! Maybe Dr. Eeek has gone crazy. Maybe he's trapped her in the canine lab. Maybe he's going to do something horrible to her — in that awful operating room!

Anyway, she must have been in the canine lab recently. How else can you explain the fact that the dog has her shoe?

"Come on," you order, pulling Sam by the arm. "We've got to go back to the canine lab. Now."

Be brave and return to the canine lab on PAGE 29.

"Larry was holding a hairbrush," you tell Dr. Eeek.

"Wrong, wrong, wrong!" he shrieks. "Obviously you're not as big a GOOSEBUMPS expert as you claim to be. Off to the Canine Maze!"

"No, please, no!" you cry. It's humiliating to act like such a wimp, especially in front of Sam. But you've got to stall. "Anything but the Canine Maze. Anything!"

"*Anything?*" Dr. Eeek asks.

Turn to PAGE 98.

You turn and run back to the door where you came in. But it's locked. You pound on it. Finally it opens.

And your mom is standing there! You know it's really her this time. The beauty mark is in the right place.

"Good work," she says, giving you a huge smile and a hug. "You figured it out. That wasn't me. That was a hologram of me that I invented. How do you like it?"

How do you like it?

Once your heart stops beating like a marching band, you like it fine! Your mom even lets you and Sam play with her hologram machine. You make hologram copies of yourselves — and leave them all over the lab.

Which is why — if you open this book to another page — you'll see yourself in Dr. Eeek's lab again. In *lots* of trouble!

Did you really think this could be . . .

THE END?

You bark and bark. Your mom smiles at you.

"Harold, I can't deal with these dogs now," she says. "I've got to find my kid." But she pats your head before she leaves.

Of course she never does find her kid — since you've been turned into a dog by the horrible Dr. Eeek.

Eventually, though, you *do* get to go home. Your mom adopts you! She takes you home and gives you plenty of dog food. Once in a while, you even get to sleep in your own bed — but only when your mom's not home. The rest of the time she makes you jump down. She doesn't want dog hairs in the bed.

The good part is that you're a *really* smart dog. *Exceptionally* smart. Because you're *not* a dog. You're a kid!

In no time, you learn great tricks. You can do things such as "go fetch a red sweater with blue buttons." You can "find the man with the black beard in the fourth row of the audience." You can add four and seven and count the answer out with your paws.

Welcome to the world of show business!

With a dog like you, your mom becomes rich and famous. She tours the world with you. And you're pretty happy. After all — being your mom's best friend isn't so bad in . . .

THE END

Dr. Eeek still has a glove on one of his hands. He moves toward you. Then pulls some of the green goo out of your mouth.

"There — you've got about two minutes until the G-substance slips back into your mouth and down your throat," he tells you with a horrible laugh. "Now, what were you saying?"

You gasp for air, then talk fast. "You worked with my mom at Eeek Labs," you say. "Until you got fired for being crazy!"

"Not at *Eeek* Labs," Dr. Eeek corrects you. "*EIK* Labs. It stands for Engineered Inner Knowledge. And yes, I did get fired. That's why I started my own lab — in the same building, just one floor above!"

"Huh?" you say, not quite understanding.

"It's simple," Herbert Wimplemeyer explains with a nasty shake of his head. "You got off the elevator on the wrong floor!"

You glance at the clock. You have only one minute left.

Quick! Turn to PAGE 21 before you choke on the goo!

"Wow," you say, shaking your head. You still can't believe this. "But how did you get here so fast?" you ask the pizza guy. "I mean, I've heard of delivery in thirty minutes. But you were here in thirty seconds!"

"Easy," he says. "Our shop is on the first floor!"

You'd like to laugh, but you don't have time. You run out into the hall to escape. You pound on the elevator button. Just then it opens — and your mom steps out! She's been searching the building for you for over an hour.

When you tell her what's happened, she calls the police immediately. She also runs down the hall and rescues Sam from the virtual reality game. Luckily, she turns it off just in time. Right before he's about to be strangled by a boa constrictor.

The police arrive a minute later and haul Dr. Eeek away.

"Whew," you say to Sam. "That was a close one. But at least it turned out all right."

"Yeah — I guess," Sam mutters, looking glum.

"What do you mean, you *guess*?" you ask. "We're safe. And we didn't get turned into something horrible in Dr. Eeek's lab. What more could you possibly want?"

"My fifty bucks!" Sam says with a goofy grin.

THE END

"It's a giant rat!" you cry.

"Are you sure?" Sam whispers. "How can a rat be that enormous?"

"How would I know?" you snap. "But it is *definitely* a rat."

You and Sam stare at the rat. The rodent is as tall as you are. You figure it must weigh over one hundred pounds. It glares at you with beady eyes. Its long whiskers twitch as it grinds two sharp front teeth.

"Let's get out of here," you tell Sam. You both turn to leave, heading for the sliding panel door.

WHAMP!

The giant rat springs forward!

It leaps in front of you. Its nails scratch the floor as it blocks the exit.

You stare at Sam. What are you going to do now? The passageway is a dead end.

The rat moves toward you. Closer and closer.

You and Sam back into a corner. The giant rat approaches. Its mouth opens wide.

"Rats," you mutter. "I think this is . . .

THE END."

You try to stay cool — even with the scientist glaring at you. You introduce yourself and Sam to the man. You reach out to shake his hand. Grown-ups usually like that.

"Ah, yes," the man says, squeezing your hand a little too tightly. "I know your mother well. A brilliant scientist."

You smile proudly.

The chimp tugs on the sleeve of the man's lab coat, trying to get his attention. He makes some signs with his hands. You can't figure out what he's trying to say — but it seems to be a kind of sign language.

The man nods, as if he understands.

"I am Professor Yzark. One of Dr. Eeek's assistants," the man says. "I see you've met Oscar." He nods toward the chimp. "Would you care to take a look at our work?"

He leads you and Sam to a wall of windows. You both peer through.

"Wow!" Sam gasps.

Take a closer look on PAGE 53.

You follow the dogs, and Sam trots along behind you.

Through the Canine Maze. Left. Right. Left. Left. You turn a dozen times. Are you ever going to get out of there? you wonder.

The pack is about twenty feet ahead of you, but all of a sudden you stop. There's a big sign on the wall up ahead. It reads EMERGENCY EXIT in big red letters. Beneath the sign is a small red button. It reads PUSH TO OPEN.

The only trouble is the button is too high for you to reach. It's four feet three inches off the ground. You start to jump, trying to push the button with your nose.

Can you do it? Here's the rule. Human beings who have been turned into dogs can jump only as high as they were tall when they were human.

If you are four feet three inches or taller, turn to PAGE 92.

If you are under four feet three inches, turn to PAGE 61.

124

"You're not my mom!" you shout, pointing at the woman in front of you. "You're a clone . . . or . . . or something!"

The woman in front of you looks exactly like your mom — except for one thing. She has a beauty mark on her right cheek. Your mom's beauty mark is on her *left* cheek!

She gives you a proud smile.

"You're right, kiddo," she says warmly. "You guessed it. I'm not your mom."

"What is she talking about?" Sam asks.

"Never mind," you answer. "It's a trick! Let's get out of here! Run!"

Run as fast as you can to PAGE 117.

You stop and give Eeek a glare that could melt stone.

"How did we get in here?" you repeat, spitting the words at him. "My mom *works* for you — you creep!"

"Your mother?" Dr. Eeek asks. He pulls himself up straight again. The twisted smile creeps back across his lips.

"Yeah," you say. "But not for long. Because I bet she'll *quit* when she hears what you tried to do to us."

"Your mother?" Dr. Eeek asks again. He sneers. "Tell me, dear child. Just what is your mother's name?"

You tell him, and he laughs. He laughs so hard that his squinty eye opens and closes. It makes him look like a hideous puppet.

Finally he stops laughing. His face turns dead serious.

"I doubt you'll ever see your mother again," he sneers with a menacing glare.

Oh, no.

"What have you done to my mom?" you cry.

Find out on PAGE 36.

126

WOOF!

That's you, barking.

Your little doggy heart is racing. You trot out into the narrow hall and run toward the approaching dogs. You're going to attack!

BARK! BARK! BARK!

They're barking as they charge toward you.

You're terrified, but you're trying to bluff. You bark as loud as you can and race to the place where the hallway turns. That way you can stand there and act as if you're protecting your territory. Maybe they'll back down. Maybe not. But it's your only chance.

Sam catches up with you and barks viciously, too. Then all at once the pack of dogs races around the corner. Their sharp teeth are bared. They're snarling. Running. Charging.

It looks as if nothing can stop them. . . .

Until they see you.

You curl back your lips, exposing your own razor-sharp teeth. You plant your feet firmly. You give a low, mean, angry growl.

GRRRRRR.

Keep growling on PAGE 46.

Luckily, you have the silver whistle. Maybe you'll get out of here alive!

The German shepherds lunge at you.

The leader is so tall that when he barks, you can feel his hot breath on your face. Suddenly his huge teeth chomp down on the neck of your T-shirt, grazing your throat!

But you don't panic.

As fast as humanly possible — which is pretty fast, since you have lightning-fast reflexes after years of playing video games — you reach into your pocket and pull out the whistle.

You blow it as hard as you can.

Nothing happens.

No sound comes out. Nothing whatsoever!

Now what are you going to do?

Face your fate on PAGE 66.

128

Your heart hammers wildly in your chest. You've got to find that antidote. Time is running out!

You yank open one lab drawer after another.

". . . sixteen, seventeen, eighteen . . ." Dr. Eeek says. Now he's toying with you, counting more slowly. His eyes are still closed.

None of the drawers contain anything that looks even remotely like an antidote to the goo. And it's taking you so long to open them. Your sticky hands cling to everything you touch.

Then you see it. In the last drawer. A jar of red gooey stuff.

Could it be?

"Twenty!" Dr. Eeek cries, opening his eyes.

You don't wait. You unscrew the lid of the jar, plunge a slimy green hand into the red stuff, and scoop out a handful.

It smells sweet, so you put it in your mouth.

"Ha ha ha!" Dr. Eeek laughs uproariously. "You think you can save your life that way? You're eating strawberry jam!"

Oh, no. He's right.

And guess what? You're allergic to strawberries!

Break out in hives on PAGE 48.

Every instinct in your body says HIDE! And Dr. Eeek's office seems like the best place.

You see it on the opposite side of the operating room. An office with a big glass window.

The sign on the door reads, EEEK'S OFFICE. KEEP OUT!

"I've got to hide!" you say to the half-boy, half-dog.

"No — don't hide," the boy warns. "Run! And take this with you."

With a flick of his wrist, he tosses you a silver whistle.

"It'll keep the dogs away," he tells you.

You start toward the door. But the footsteps are right outside.

Uh-oh. Time to make another choice.

If you follow the boy's advice, run to PAGE 112.

If you think it's best to turn around and hide in Dr. Eeek's office, turn to PAGE 34.

130

Cautiously, you continue straight ahead in the maze. You and Sam walk side by side. But the hallway is so narrow, you just barely fit.

"Hey, quit bumping me," Sam snaps. He shoves you aside with his shoulder.

"I didn't bump you," you reply. "Quit bumping *me*."

"Ouch!" Sam says as he slams into the wall beside him.

Uh-oh. You suddenly figure it out. The corridor is gradually getting narrower. In fact, as you gaze ahead, it seems to narrow down to nothing. It almost looks as if the two walls come together at a point.

"Maybe we should turn around and go back," Sam suggests. "This is a dead end."

A dead end? Your throat tightens up at the thought.

You check behind you to see if anyone — or anything — is back there.

That doggy smell is getting stronger.

What do you want to do?

Keep going to the end of the narrowing hall on PAGE 62.

Or turn around and go back to the fork on PAGE 87.

About the Author

R.L. STINE is the author of over three dozen best-selling thrillers and mysteries for young people. Recent titles for teenagers include *I Saw You That Night!*, *Call Waiting*, *Halloween Night II*, *The Dead Girlfriend*, and *The Baby-sitter IV*, all published by Scholastic. He is also the author of the *Fear Street* series.

Bob lives in New York City with his wife, Jane, and fifteen-year-old son, Matt.

Pick a Scare. Any Scare.

Goosebumps®

Tim Swanson loves magic tricks.
Someday he wants to be a real
magician like his hero, Amaz-O.
But when Tim goes to see his
hero's show, he ends up stealing
Amaz-O's bag of tricks.
Secret tricks. Scary tricks.
And one mean rabbit who's got
more than a few of those tricks
up his sleeve.

Bad Hare Day
Goosebumps #41
by R.L. Stine

Appearing in a bookstore near you!

GBT795

GET
Goosebumps®
by R.L. Stine

☐ BAB48346-3	#34 Revenge of the Lawn Gnomes	$3.50
☐ BAB48340-4	#35 A Shocker on Shock Street	$3.50
☐ BAB56873-6	#36 The Haunted Mask II	$3.99
☐ BAB56874-4	#37 The Headless Ghost	$3.99
☐ BAB56875-2	#38 The Abominable Snowman of Pasadena	$3.99
☐ BAB56876-0	#39 How I Got My Shrunken Head	$3.99
☐ BAB56877-9	#40 Night of the Living Dummy III	$3.99
☐ BAB56644-X	Goosebumps 1996 Calendar	$9.95
☐ BAB62836-4	Book & Light Set: Tales to Give You The Creeps - Ten Spooky Stories	$11.95
☐ BAB26603-9	Book & Light Set #2: More Tales to Give You Goosebumps	$11.95
☐ BAB55323-2	Give Yourself Goosebumps Book #1: Escape from the Carnival of Horrors	$3.50
☐ BAB56645-8	Give Yourself Goosebumps Book #2: Tick Tock, You're Dead	$3.99
☐ BAB56646-6	Give Yourself Goosebumps Book #3: Trapped in Bat Wing Hall	$3.99
☐ BAB53770-9	The Goosebumps Monster Blood Pack	$11.95
☐ BAB50995-0	The Goosebumps Monster Sound Chip Book	$12.95
☐ BAB60265-9	Goosebumps Official Collector's Caps Collecting Kit	$5.99

Scare me, thrill me, mail me GOOSEBUMPS now!

Available wherever you buy books, or use this order form. Scholastic Inc., P.O. Box 7502, 2931 East McCarty Street, Jefferson City, MO 65102

Please send me the books I have checked above. I am enclosing $_____ (please add $2.00 to cover shipping and handling). Send check or money order — no cash or C.O.D.s please.

Name _____Age _____

Address _____

City _____State/Zip _____

Please allow four to six weeks for delivery. Offer good in the U.S. only. Sorry, mail orders are not available to residents of Canada. Prices subject to change.

GB795